Elvis and the Dearly Departed

**Center Point
Large Print**

**This Large Print Book carries the
Seal of Approval of N.A.V.H.**

Elvis and the Dearly Departed

Peggy Webb

CENTER POINT PUBLISHING
THORNDIKE, MAINE

This Center Point Large Print edition
is published in the year 2009 by arrangement with
Kensington Publishing Corp.

The text of this Large Print edition is unabridged.
In other aspects, this book may vary
from the original edition.
Printed in the United States of America.
Set in 16-point Times New Roman type.

ISBN: 978-1-60285-344-7

Library of Congress Cataloging-in-Publication Data

Webb, Peggy.
  Elvis and the dearly departed / Peggy Webb.
    p. cm.
  ISBN 978-1-60285-344-7 (library binding : alk. paper)
  1. Basset hound--Fiction. 2. Mississippi--Social life and customs--Fiction.
    3. Large type books. I. Title.

PS3573.E1985E58 2009
813'.54--dc22

2008033181

For Cecilia, Susan, David, and William,
with love from your Gigi

Elvis' Opinion # I on the Valentine Family, Zen Buddhism, and Leftover T-bone Steak

Nobody asks my opinion around here, but if they did I'd tell them basset hounds are the most brilliant dogs on earth. We could rule the world if they'd let us. Of course, around here I'm lucky if I get to rule over the oak tree I consider my private pissing post. After all, I was the first dog on these premises, and if you ask me that makes me the King. Not to mention the fact that I had umpteen hit records in my other life as a fat man in a white sequined jumpsuit.

I guess you're thinking I'm one of those modern-day reincarnationists, but I'm not. I'm Baptist to the bone. Give me hellfire and damnation anytime over all that New Age stuff. Callie Valentine Jones—that's my human mom—claims to be Zen Buddhist. Burns candles and chants stuff under full moons and all that mumbo jumbo. But I think that's because she's just looking everywhere for answers to all the stuff she has to deal with. Her inconvenient attraction to her almost ex, for one thing.

That would be my human daddy, Jack. They had a falling-out over his Harley Screamin' Eagle with the heated seats. Take it from me—those seats feel mighty good on a nasty day in January when temperatures in Tupelo, Mississippi (my birthplace, population forty thousand), drop below forty.

I'm partial, myself, to hot weather. Lazy August days like today. Brings out the best in me. I can lie in the shade and let my ears flap in the breeze. Nobody would notice one is longer than the other, which has kept me from winning more Best in Show titles than I care to think about. But what's a dog show title when you're already the King?

Back to the Valentines . . . Callie's mama is always teetering on the brink of financial doom. Personally I admire a woman gutsy enough to place a fifty-dollar bet on a five-dollar hand. It's not as if Ruby Nell's addicted or anything. She just likes an occasional jaunt to Tunica, where casinos sprang up out of the cotton patch like strangler kudzu after the Mississippi legislature had a big brain fart and legalized gambling. That's all right, Mama! I sang some of my biggest hits in the casinos of Las Vegas.

And then there's Lovie. Aptly named. She's had more lovers than I've had fleas. Callie worries needlessly over her cousin's affairs. Any woman who can build a catering business out of recipes featuring whiskey and sherry deserves the motto *love me tender.* And any other way she wants it.

Some say Callie's uncle Charlie is the only stable, sensible member of the family. Granted, he is her rock of ages. But let me tell you, before Lovie's daddy settled down to making the dead

8

look like they can sit up and walk over at Eternal Rest Funeral Home (pronounced *E*-ternal around here), Charlie Valentine was conducting a colorful life that narrowly kept him from singing the jailhouse rock. A man after my own heart. Give him a sequined jumpsuit and some sideburns and he'd still set hearts aflutter, even at sixty-two.

Well, now. What's this I hear?

It'll never make a number-one hit record, but it's music to my ears. Callie, calling me to supper. Judging by the smells that have been coming from the grill, I'd say it's a good leftover T-bone steak.

Thank you, thank you very much. Elvis has left the building.

Obituaries

Tupelo—Dr. Leonard Laton, 78, prominent physician, died Wednesday, August 8, at Peaceful Pines Nursing Home after an extended illness. He is predeceased by his wife, Marie Hotchins Laton.

Survivors include one son, Kevin Laton of Tupelo; three daughters, Janice Laton Mims and her husband, Bradford, San Francisco; Bevvie Laton, Boulder; and Mellie Laton, Tupelo; and three step-grandchildren also of San Francisco.

Eternal Rest Funeral Home is handling all arrangements, which are incomplete at this time.

Chapter 1

Love, Vodka, and Red Pasties

Elvis has just peed on my shoes, which is my life in a nutshell. Every time I think I'm fixing to forge forward, somebody comes along to rain on my parade.

Not only do I have the most arrogant failed show dog east of the Mississippi, but I have a beauty parlor that's more outgo than income, an almost ex-husband I'm fighting for custody of my dog and my inconvenient libido, and a mama who makes withdrawals as if I'm the Bank of Callie Valentine Jones.

Currently Elvis is taking umbrage over getting dog chow for supper while Dr. Laton's California relatives eat all the T-bone steak. Uncle Charlie always offers the out-of-town bereaved a place to stay, and my two-story, white clapboard house in Mooreville (population six hundred and fifty) on the outskirts of Tupelo is the only one in the Valentine family big enough to accommodate Janice Laton Mims, her husband, Bradford, and his three teenaged boys, plus Janice's seven-piece matched set of Louis Vuitton luggage. The only good thing I can say about the invasion is that I don't have to worry about being bushwhacked in my own bed by Jack Jones.

I bend over to scratch behind Elvis' ears. Ordinarily this would make him forgive me, but just when I'm about to placate my opinionated basset hound, one of Dr. Laton's step-grandkids— Rufus, I think—runs up and pulls his tail. Major mistake. Elvis prances over and hikes his leg on Janice Laton Mims's Prada purse.

"Somebody get that animal out of here," she yells, never mind that she's a guest in my house.

"Don't worry. I'll clean it up. It'll be just like new." Collaring her purse and my dog, I escape to my kitchen.

Some people don't know the meaning of gratitude.

I'm happy to say I'm not among that number. I'm putting up with the Laton bunch because it makes Uncle Charlie happy, and I'd do anything for the man who has been my surrogate father and my stronghold for most of my thirty-seven years.

His motto at Eternal Rest is *"laissez le bon temps rouler,"* which sounds strange for a funeral home unless you know the Valentine family. Although we have our serious side, we believe in letting the good times roll through every stage of life and that includes the leave-taking. Mama provides jazzy music and fancy headstones, I do the deceased's hair and makeup, Lovie eases the bereaved's pain with dishes featuring vodka, and Uncle Charlie sends the dearly departed off in high style to that big tent revival in the sky—or in the opposite direction.

14

The Valentine family has death covered. What we don't have covered is keeping our own leaky boats afloat, especially in the treacherous waters of finance and love.

As if to prove my point, Lovie calls my cell phone while I'm in the middle of trying to rescue the overpriced purse.

"Callie, you've got to stall Daddy on Dr. Laton's family viewing."

"Why?"

"Because Kevin Laton's going to be a little bit late."

"How late?"

"I don't know. It depends on how excited he gets over my crotchless panties and how long he can hold out."

Lovie's the most outrageous woman I know. She can walk into a room and bring everybody to their knees with laughter. But there's so much more to her than entertainment value. She's a strong, resilient, one-woman comfort machine.

Every time life clips my wings, Lovie picks me up and lets me glide along in her tailwinds till I'm strong enough to fly again.

After Daddy accidentally drove his tractor into the Tombigee River and floated off to Glory Land, I holed up in my bedroom determined to become the only ten-year-old recluse in Mooreville. Even Mama couldn't get me to come out. But Lovie marched into my bedroom and

15

said, "If you don't come outside and play wedding Barbies this instant, I'm going to quit wearing clothes."

"Nobody in this house cares, Lovie," I told her.

"I bet the preacher will. Next Sunday I'm going to church naked."

And she would have, too. Even at nine, she was as bullheaded as the team of mules Granddaddy Valentine used to plow the vegetable garden. I left my malaise behind and didn't pick it up again till Jack left. Lovie came straight over with a six-pack of Hershey's bars and an armful of *I Love Lucy* DVDs, and brought me back to life.

If I had her capacity for cures, I'd save her from her bad choices in men.

But I don't, so all I can do is tell her, "Kevin's a playboy. He's never going to settle down."

"Who said I wanted to settle down? Besides, you married God's gift to women and look where that got you."

A yearlong standoff in the divorce court. That's where. Over a fracas involving the Harley that I refuse to discuss.

"That's tacky of you to remind me, Lovie."

"I'm a tacky, shallow person," she says, which is the exact opposite of the truth. "Just do this one thing for me, Callie, and I'll take Elvis to the vet the next time he has to go."

Taking Elvis to the vet is my personal Battle at Waterloo. He hikes his leg on everything from the car tires to the vet's pants leg, and that's when he's in a good mood.

"All right. I'll stall."

I make this promise reluctantly, not because stalling will be hard to do—the way the Laton teenagers are ripping around my backyard it'll take a lasso to get them started on the fifteen-minute drive to Eternal Rest in Tupelo—but because I worry about Lovie. She can't say no. More than one man has mixed up the name of her catering business—Lovie's Luscious Eats—and called it Luscious Lovie Eats.

She's the only woman I know who can make a hundred and ninety pounds look like a bombshell.

Beside her I look like a swizzle stick. No butt, long, skinny legs, size 34-B bra, which I refuse to stuff with push-up pads no matter how much sexier Lovie thinks I'd be. It's not sex I'm aiming for; it's commitment. Love everlasting and a house full of children.

Of course, my eggs are drying up even as I speak. If Jack keeps me hostage in the divorce courts much longer, I can forget progeny.

I'm getting ready to head outside and round up the California Latons when Mama calls from her monument company.

"Callie, I thought you and that California bunch were headed up here to pick up Mellie Laton. That mousy little tightwad is driving me crazy. It's time for my bedtime toddy."

17

"It's just five thirty, Mama."

"It's bedtime somewhere. First, Mellie picked out the cheapest monument on the lot. Then she wanted me to have it engraved with *rest in peace.* As if I'd ruin the entire reputation of Everlasting Monuments just because she has no imagination."

Mama's a colorful woman, partial to neon-pink caftans featuring Hawaiian flowers and tombstone engravings that proclaim *He boogied on up to heaven* and *Saint Peter's holding the trumpet solo for Leonard Laton.*

"Where is she now?" I ask.

"Sitting on my genuine Naugahyde couch in her ugly brown shoes drinking all my coffee and complaining because it's not Colombian. I'm going stark, raving mad. What I need is a little restorative trip to Tunica. You don't happen to have five hundred cash lying around, do you?"

"As I recall you didn't pay back the last hundred I loaned you."

"This time it'll be different. I feel a winning streak coming on."

What I feel is another big hole in my finances. I know I ought to be sensible and say no, but I never can refuse Mama. Ever since Daddy died, I've been trying to make up his loss to Ruby Nell Valentine.

Of course, she has to me, too. Even a little hint that I'm blue, and she races to the piano and belts out "Side by Side" in her lusty contralto. Then she

18

hugs me and says, "As long as we've got each other, kid, we're okay."

I believe her. She'd never win anybody's Mother of the Year Award, but she has taught me to value the things that really count—family, friends, and a faithful dog.

"All right, Mama," I tell her now. "But just one more time."

"I promise."

Pigs are likely to grow wings and fly before Mama keeps that promise, and both of us know it. But we laugh and pretend otherwise because that's the Southern way: look on the bright side, no matter what.

One hour, two BC powders, and an act of God later—a big thunderclap that has driven the California Latons inside—I'm in Uncle Charlie's office at Eternal Rest.

"You look a bit frazzled, dear heart," Uncle Charlie tells me.

When he hugs me it's like being embraced by a combination of Santa Claus and a Sicilian godfather who wouldn't hesitate to cut off the head of an enemy's prized racehorse and put it in his bed.

"I'm fine, Uncle Charlie." Not exactly the truth, but I don't like to worry him. He takes his job as head of the Valentine family seriously.

"If all the Latons are here, we'll commence."

"Everybody's here except Bevvie."

19

"And where is she?"

"Hunting big game in the African bush with an arsenal of weapons that would make the U.S. Army green with envy." Lovie struts into the office sporting a hickey on her neck and a hairdo that looks like it was styled by a Mix Master. Red. Titian number six. Compliments of yours truly. "I pumped the information out of Kevin."

"Well, good for you, sweetheart."

Uncle Charlie offers both of us an arm, and if he's aware of Lovie's double entendre, we'll never know. He can win your new Cadillac in a poker game and make you think he's doing you a favor, wear a fifty-dollar suit and make you believe it's designer, show off a niece and a daughter with a dubious family tree and make you think we're blue-blooded aristocracy. "Shall we go into the viewing room and unveil the good doctor?"

The Latons are waiting for us in the sitting area off the viewing room. The rowdy Mims teenagers are lined up like bowling pins behind their daddy, Bradford, the middle-aged jock type, who has his hand on his wife's shoulder. Janice Laton Mims showed more emotion over her defaced Prada purse than she's showing over her deceased daddy. Of course, it could be her facelift. Her skin's stretched so tight she can hardly blink, let alone move her mouth.

Mellie, too, is composed—her patent leather purse clutched in her lap, lips and legs pressed tightly together. Wearing glasses that went out of style with Herbert Hoover, she looks like she wouldn't say boo to a fence post.

And I won't even comment on the doctor's adopted son, Kevin. A hunk, granted. Lovie naturally gravitates toward brawn.

Uncle Charlie seats Lovie and me in two wing-back chairs, then moves to the front of the room.

"Dr. Leonard Laton was a brilliant man and an asset to our town. It's an honor to assist you in making his journey to the hereafter memorable."

Leading us into the viewing room, Uncle Charlie sweeps open the casket to display the late doctor in his final splendor.

Janice screams, Mellie faints, and Kevin says, "I didn't know the old boy still had it in him."

In plain view on Dr. Laton's chest is a pair of red sequined pasties.

Uncle Charlie slams the lid shut. While I fan Mellie, Lovie plucks the pasties out of the casket.

"I was wondering where I left those." Any fool can see she's lying. These pasties wouldn't fit Lovie's fist, let alone the ballistic missiles she likes to show off with low-cut blouses. "I was in the casket trying it out for size."

"Kinky," Kevin says, and Janice whacks him with her Prada purse.

"I'm sure Uncle Charlie will get to the bottom of this," I say. "Meanwhile, the powder rooms are right down the hall. After we freshen up we'll retire to the reception room for some of Lovie's good food."

Janice perks up at this information. No self-respecting survivor would put Kentucky Fried chicken and potato salad featuring mustard on the table when they can have shrimp jambalaya, grits soufflé, and Prohibition punch made by the most famous caterer in Tupelo, if not the whole state of Mississippi.

I leave the Laton sisters in the powder room pressing wet handkerchiefs to their foreheads and putting on hot-pink lipstick that doesn't match a thing they're wearing. Then I race toward the kitchen.

Lovie tosses me a bottle of bourbon. "Quick, Callie, dump some in."

"Where?"

"Everywhere." She's emptying a vodka bottle into the punch and I pour in the bourbon.

If we're lucky the Latons won't even remember their names tonight, let alone that the late Dr. Laton was in possession of a set of red pasties complete with tassels.

Dr. Laton's funeral will be memorable, all right. But for all the wrong reasons.

Chapter 2

Hairdos, Body Heat, and Bubbles Malone

After yesterday's fracas at the funeral home, it's a relief to go to work.

I never meant to settle here in spite of the local saying, "When you die, if you're lucky you go to Mooreville, Mississippi." After college I was going to move to Atlanta, make a life for myself as wife, mother, and pillar of the community, and a name for myself as a hairstylist.

But Mama had to have knee surgery, and my best friend and cohort in crime (as Lovie and I call ourselves) had started a catering business she didn't want to leave. Plus, this great little shop came up for sale.

This is my domain, the one little segment of my life that's completely manageable. I renamed the shop Hair.Net and installed a manicurist's station (sans manicurist, which I can never afford until I pay off my mortgage and my credit card bill at Lucky's Designer Shoes).

Mama's Everlasting Monuments is conveniently located next door (or inconveniently, depending on the day).

Now I'm here rolling the hair of one of my regulars, while Elvis snoozes nearby.

Personally I'd prefer to be giving Bitsy a modern cut and a blow-dry, but I pride myself on three things: keeping my mouth shut, satisfying my customers, and wearing cute shoes.

This is life as I know and love it. Outside, a Peterbilt rig puts on air brakes at Mooreville's one and only four-way stop, the King's hit "All Shook Up" blares from the video store next door on my right, and Elvis rouses from his nap in the sunshine by the front door to howl.

"Good Lord." Bitsy covers her ears, and Elvis, sniffing with disdain, sashays toward the break room and the comfort of his duck-down doggie bed.

In this lazy ebb and flow of my days I can almost forget that I lost Jack Jones to a Harley, my prospects of children and financial solvency get dimmer every day, and the California Latons are sleeping off Lovie's punch in my upstairs guest bedroom.

Mama breezes in with a five-hundred-dollar plate of brownies. That's the way I've learned to look at the loans I make to subsidize her predilection for poker chips.

I give her the cash and she gives me a hug. Plus, unsolicited advice.

"Honey, now that you've cut Jack loose, women are drooling all over him."

She worships the quicksand he walks on.

"Mama, I don't care." Unfortunately, this is not

true. "Don't forget to shut the back door on your way out."

By the time Mama and my last morning customer leave I'm four hundred and twenty dollars in the hole.

On the bright side, I don't have anybody to answer to and so far Elvis hasn't peed on my favorite shoes, a cute little bronze and silver pair of Salvatore Ferragamo sandals that lace around my ankles and make my legs look longer than Julia Roberts'.

"Elvis? Are you ready for lunch?"

Usually the mention of food brings him running.

A quick check shows his bed empty, his second-favorite spot under the washbasin vacant, and the back door wide open. Running around the small yard yelling for my dog, I see my custody battle turning in favor of Jack.

Panicked, I race inside and dial his cell phone. He answers on the first ring and I don't know whether to come clean about Elvis or cry.

I do both.

"Sit tight, I'm on the way."

Holy cow! Now here I am, my good intentions and my willpower taking a powder while the man who knows how to turn every surface in my beauty parlor into a pleasure playground roars this way with eight hundred pounds of horsepower between his legs. I might as well strip and throw myself across the pink vinyl cushions on my love seat.

With the distant roar of his Screamin' Eagle putting goose bumps the size of hen eggs all over me, I make a mental list of every reason I should hate him.

There are about eight hundred and seventy-five, so this could take a while. Topping the list is that I don't even know who he is. Sure, he says he's an international business consultant named Jack Jones, but he also said—in French, mind you—that his parents were diplomats in Paris and couldn't come to the wedding, which proved to be a big fat lie. Turns out he's an orphan who was such a hell-raiser, nobody would adopt him. And I didn't find that out until three years after I'd said *I do*.

On the eve of my thirtieth birthday, just when I despaired of ever finding a hero, Jack Jones rolled into Mooreville in a silver Jag and started spreading money and charm like it was oil and he was a rich Texan. Which is one of the many states he claims to hail from. Texas. Idaho. New Hampshire. North Dakota. Georgia. Maine. And he can speak in every one of the accents. Plus Spanish, Italian, German, and Japanese in addition to French.

He seduced me in six languages, then tied me in a knot and delivered me to the altar with the promise of house, dog, and family. He delivered the house (my current abode, which, thank goodness, he's not fighting for) and the dog (Elvis, whom he'll get over my dead body).

"When I can settle down we'll have kids,' kept telling me. Then he proceeded to run all over the country doing Lord knows what.

"You look good enough to eat," he says, and I nearly jump out of my skin.

There he stands—Jack Jones in the tightest black jeans I've ever seen, a black T-shirt that shows every muscle he's got and a bulge in his pants that's either "happy to see me" or his Colt .45.

"Don't you even try."

He bends me backward over the love seat, then runs his left hand over my lips, down my neck, and into the front of my blouse while I'm trying to decide whether to slap his face or unzip his pants.

"As tempting as you are, I have other things on my mind today, Callie. Finding my dog, for one." He releases me and I land in a heap on the love seat. "How did you lose him?"

"That's just like you, Jack. Standing there making accusations instead of finding Elvis. He could be in Timbuktu by now."

"Not the way he moves. Come on." We head outside and he tosses me a helmet. "Put that on."

"I'm not getting on that Harley."

He picks me up, tosses me aboard, then roars off while I hang on. If I could hit the side of a barn, I'd shoot him. With my blue jean skirt hiked up past decency, I look like a gun moll. And I don't even want to think about my Ferragamo sandals. The left one has come untied. It'll probably catch in the jerk me off, and smash me against the _____. I'll look like roadkill. Even Uncle Charlie won't be able to repair the damage.

I don't have much time to worry because Jack comes to a screeching halt at one of Elvis' favorite haunts, Fayrene's convenience store, Gas, Grits, and Guts. (She added the Guts part after she started selling fish bait.) Usually she has a flea market going in the parking lot and kids hanging around, happy to share a hot dog and scratch behind the ears of a dog who thinks he's famous.

"Nope," Fayrene tells us after we inquire about Elvis. "I haven't seen hide nor hair of him. But I've been so torn up I wouldn't have noticed a herd of elephants. I'm suffering from acid reflex and fireballs in my useless."

Translated, that's acid reflux and fibroids in the uterus. Fayrene is Mama's best friend and the queen of malapropisms and green polyester. I've tried to steer her to a more flattering color but she says she likes green because it's the color of money.

I console her over her imaginary ailments and she says, "I'm glad to see you're back with Jack."

Jack winks at her. "So am I."

I flounce out and straddle the hated Harley. "I'm not back with you."

"Not yet."

He revs up and we check the rest of Elvis' stomping ground: the Mooreville High School ball field where he loves to sit on the sidelines and howl along with the band or watch ball practice, the barbershop that features a red-and-white-striped pole he regularly anoints, and the used car lot whose owner has a big black 1960s Cadillac that Elvis considers his.

All these places are within easy walking distance of Hair.Net. Mooreville is not much more than a wide place in the road. Two roads, actually. The four-way stop in the heart of things is at the intersection of Highways 178 and 371. That's not saying much because both are two-lane roads.

If the state ever adds more lanes I'll be too worried to buy shoes. My dog is an escape artist. If a hound dog wants to wander, even my almost-ex can't keep it fenced in.

"We might as well go back," I say.

"There's another place I want to check out."

We peel out of the used car lot, race four miles south on 371, and hang a hard right on the narrow lane across from Wildwood Chapel Cemetery, dominated by Daddy's black African marble obelisk, Aunt Minrose's (Lovie's mom) soaring pink Italian marble angel, and our Valentine grandparents' replica of the Pearly Gates.

Jack screeches to a halt in a wooded glade overlooking Mama's lake on the hundred-and-sixty-acre farm where I grew up.

Dreams gestate in the beauty of this land. When we were sixteen Lovie and I sat side by side on an overhanging limb of the massive blackjack oak and planned our futures. At the age of eighty, she was to be an even more famous musician than her mother, while I was going to be in my own house surrounded by sixteen great-grandchildren, an adoring husband, and a faithful dog.

At the rate I'm going, the only part I'm going to end up with is a faithful dog.

Now I'm telling Jack, "Oh no, you don't," but he just grins and plucks me off the Harley.

The minute my feet touch that beloved, almost sacred ground, I'm a goner. And I can't say I'm all that sorry, either.

Much, *much* later, as I brush grass off my skirt I tell Jack, "Don't think this means you're going to get custody of Elvis."

He swats me on the butt, tosses me onto his Harley, and roars off.

But I'm not fixing to start feeling guilty. Love makes fools of us all, and that's all I'm saying on that subject. Besides, dallying with my ex is better than being roadkill.

"Callie, you have grass in your hair." Lovie's sharp blue eyes never miss a thing.

"Oh, shoot." I reach up and brush the bits and pieces out, hopefully before Uncle Charlie or any of the Latons notice.

We're in the boardroom at Eternal Rest where Grover Grimsley, who happens to be my divorce lawyer, is setting up a screen so we can watch Dr. Laton deliver funeral instructions as well as his last will and testament.

"Jack?" Lovie asks.

"How'd you know?"

"You're predictable. And he's just downright dangerous, which is why he still rings every one of your chimes."

"I want a steady man with a decent nine-to-five job."

"I'd amputate my G-spot with a shish kebab stick before I'd have a man that boring. And so would you."

"Hush up, Lovie. Grover will hear you."

"I wonder if he's partial to cream puffs."

Lovie and I slide into seats at the back so we can spy.

When I arrived at Eternal Rest with a beard burn located where I'll never tell and a nagging fear about Elvis, Uncle Charlie told me, "I want you and Lovie to observe everybody. It had to be one of the Latons who surprised us with the pasties, because they were the only ones here besides us."

Now Uncle Charlie's up front saying, "It looks like everybody is here."

"Not quite." Grover looks at his watch, then at the back door.

As if she's been waiting for her cue, an aging Amazonian peroxided blonde strolls in wearing widow's weeds that show enough bare leg and cleavage to scandalize everybody in the Bible Belt. Lifting the veil of her sassy sequined hat with one black-gloved hand, she winks at me, which is a pure miracle. She's wearing so much mascara it's a wonder she can move her eyes.

"Do you mind?" the woman asks, then sits beside me, crosses her legs, and proceeds to dangle a sling-backed shoe with killer stiletto heels. Her fragrance wafts over me in a nauseating wave—Poison.

Lovie punches me in the ribs and I punch her back while Grover says, "Let's proceed."

He dims the lights and switches on the DVD video player and up pops a larger-than-life image of Dr. Leonard Laton.

"Well, I guess you're all here except Bevvie, who is probably off shooting something, which means I'm dead and all of you can breathe a sigh of relief. Janice, stop your silly histrionics, and, Mellie, you never did give a damn about me, so don't start pretending now."

Janice leans on her husband's shoulder in a fake swoon I can spot a mile away while Mellie sits stiff-backed. The woman beside me takes a man's handkerchief with a monogrammed M out of a black sequined evening bag.

"You're in good hands with my buddy Charlie Valentine, who's not only the best undertaker in Mississippi but the best fisherman. Much as it will pain all of you to hang around and look at my car-

32

cass, I'm not fixing to be put in the ground till every one of you is here. And I don't want a single one of you crying at my funeral."

"How could he?" Janice yells, but when her husband rises to escort her from the room, she jerks his coattail, and he plops back into his chair.

As if he had anticipated her reaction, Dr. Laton says, "You didn't shed a tear nor lift a hand while I wasted away at Peaceful Pines Nursing Home. For that reason and many more that are none of your damned business, I leave my house in Tupelo, my condo in Key West, three million dollars in stocks and mutual funds, and my Mercedes Benz to Bubbles Malone."

The woman beside me smothers a sound with her handkerchief that might be mistaken for grief if you weren't sitting elbow to elbow.

"Bubbles, strut your stuff, honey, and finish scandalizing this greedy bunch." Dr. Laton laughs before he fades to silence.

Bubbles rises on a wave of Poison and takes a turn around the room that makes Gypsy Rose Lee look like Mary Poppins. She stops in front of Bradford, strips off one of her long black gloves, and playfully pops him on the leg.

"This is an outrage." Janice lunges out of her seat, and I'll swear if Bradford hadn't restrained his wife, she might have clawed six inches of pancake makeup off Bubbles' face.

"Janice, what are we going to do?" Mellie asks.

"Break the will, you fool."

As Bubbles settles back beside me, the image of Dr. Laton flickers, then becomes clear again. "Did I say *being of sound mind?* If not, put it in your pipe and smoke it. There's not a lawyer in the U.S. who can prove me mentally incompetent. Kevin, you're the only member of my family who didn't act like I was some kind of horse's ass. I know you'll probably squander it, but I'm leaving you a million dollars."

Kevin surprises me by taking the news without revealing a single emotion.

"The rest of my estate is to be equally divided between Peaceful Pines and whatever charities Grover Grimsley sees fit. Now if you'll excuse me, I have an appointment with the devil."

As Dr. Laton vanishes from the screen, the Warner Brothers' Looney Tunes cartoon logo comes up. For a while the only sound we hear is the raucous laughter of Woody Woodpecker.

Then the room explodes.

"This will take two gallons of Prohibition punch." Lovie hustles toward the kitchen with Kevin in her wake.

While Uncle Charlie and Grover Grimsley form a flank between the Laton women and the outrageous beneficiary and I desperately search for ways to affect a truce, Bubbles Malone vanishes.

Elvis' Opinion # 2 on Las Vegas, French Poodles, and Taking Care of Business

I guess you're wondering how I could walk out on Callie since she's one of the truest hearts I know and I live by the creed *don't be cruel.* I could tell you I took advantage of the wide-open back door in the hopes my human mom and dad would get back together, but the truth is, every now and then a dog has to take care of business.

I'd planned on sniffing Ruby Nell's tombstones, maybe marking a few, then ambling over to Gas, Grits, and Guts to see if anybody had left a half-empty box of fish bait. After that I was going back to the beauty shop before Callie missed me. But I got sidetracked by Bubbles Malone. I could smell big city all over her even before I sneaked in as she went inside to ask for directions to Eternal Rest. Fayrene quizzed her within an inch of her size 36-D push-up bra.

Don't ask how I know the size. Just trust me. And every bit of it was real.

When Bubbles mentioned she used to perform at Caesar's Palace, I sidled up hoping she'd recognize me and ask for my paw print. But she didn't. I should have known a woman too vain to put on the reading glasses I saw when she dropped that little bitty purse would miss her golden opportunity.

Now, I knew if she went strutting into Eternal Rest showing off those knockers, the Valentines would be all shook-up. I fully intended to mosey on back to the beauty parlor and warn Callie.

But fate intervened. The prettiest little French poodle this side of Hollywood and Vine sashayed by exuding pheromones you could smell all the way to the Alabama state line. Well, bless'a my soul!

I seized the first opportunity to dash out the door. Then I sucked in my paunch and marched right up to her.

"I'm Elvis," I drawled, "and I can fly you to moon."

A basset hound or even a Jack Russell terrier would have known I stole that line from another singer, but a French poodle in heat will believe anything you tell her.

She blinked her big brown eyes at me and I was a goner. We trotted off to find some privacy and lost all track of time.

Now I'm lying here behind the Mooreville Truck Stop with Ann Margret curled up beside me snoozing. Turns out she had the same opinion of me as John Lennon. "Before Elvis there was nothing." I feel the urge to kick up my heels and howl at the full moon.

But in spite of all the stories you've heard to the contrary, I'm smarter than that. Instead of giving away our love nest, I amble over to the back door of the kitchen and find some good scraps of country-fried steak, black-eyed peas and corn bread.

It's not the fried peanut butter and banana sandwiches I was so fond of before I fell from Graceland, but it's still good Southern home cooking.

Well, back to my foxy little poodle. TCB, baby!

Elvis' Recipe for Fried Peanut Butter and Banana Sandwiches

First, watch Callie toast two pieces of white bread. I know whole wheat's better for you, but a dog sweating under an August sun hotter than stage lights needs all the carbohydrates and sugar he can get.

Sit there and drool while she melts about half a stick of butter (the real kind, not that cheap imitation stuff) in the bottom of a skillet. Next, howl "How Great Thou Art" while she spreads smooth peanut butter on one side of the toast, puts a bunch of sliced bananas in the middle, and fries the sandwich, turning it till it's golden brown on both sides.

Dig a nice cool hole under the oak tree and bury the sandwich until you can sneak off, dig it up, and enjoy it without being bothered by Callie's silly stray cats and that dumb cocker spaniel she found in the Dumpster behind the video store.

Chapter 3

Feuds, Hot Fudge,
and Moveable Corpses

The funeral home is a war zone. Mellie's not speaking to Janice, Janice is not speaking to Bradford, the teenagers are not speaking to anybody but their newly rich uncle, Kevin's not speaking to Lovie (who turned down a proposal while she was backed up against the refrigerator in Eternal Rest), and nobody in the Laton family is speaking to Uncle Charlie.

All he said was, "You probably want to see your daddy before you leave the funeral home."

"You can hang his sorry carcass out for the birds," Janice said, then drove her Avis rental car off and left Bradford and the boys to hitchhike back to Mooreville.

I was getting ready to offer a ride, but thank goodness Mellie said she'd drive them back.

Frankly, I'm tired of the Latons. All I want to do is find Elvis and a quiet place to curl up and repent my latest transgression with my ex. I always do this, say I'm not going to feel the least bit guilty, then have second thoughts and figure a woman headed to battle in the divorce court ought to know better than to sleep with the enemy.

After the warring camps leave, I grab my purse. "Uncle Charlie, is there anything I can do before I go?"

"No, dear heart. I'm going by Grover's office to discuss the progress he's made on finding Bevvie Laton. Then I'm driving out to the farm to fix Ruby Nell's front porch glider."

Mama will be sorry she missed him. It serves her right for gambling away my money.

Uncle Charlie locks up and we walk into the full blast of hundred-degree August heat. All I can say is it's good for business. Nobody can keep a hairdo more than two hours in this humidity. Except me. I'm proud to say my slick brown bob can withstand tornadoes and still look like I stepped out of *Vogue*.

"Lovie, leave your van here and ride with me. Elvis is missing, and I want to find him."

Without a single question, Lovie hefts herself into my maroon four-wheel-drive pickup, which is my alter ego. If I could be a truck I'd want to be a take-charge Dodge Ram with a kick-ass Hemi engine. Nobody messes with this sucker.

I pull out of the parking lot and head to the east side of town toward the King's birthplace.

Every time we pass by, Elvis howls. Tupelo Hardware, too, for that matter. On the corner of Front Street and Main, it still looks very much the way it did when Gladys Presley bought her son's first guitar. The owners have marked a big X on the spot where he stood and love to claim credit for starting him on the road to fame. As a tribute to the King, the store keeps a fading cardboard poster in the window of a young, skinny Elvis caught in swivel-hipped splendor.

They sell Elvis guitars, too, and I'm not ashamed to admit I have one. Jack was going to teach me to play it, but we all know how that turned out.

Lovie and I are bumping across the railroad tracks east of the hardware store when my cell phone rings. She digs it out of my purse.

"It's Jack."

"Tell him I'm not talking to him. Permanently."

She hands me the phone.

"Hello, Jack. Why aren't you out chasing women?" Mama's innuendo at work.

"You're the only woman I want to chase and I'm still looking for Elvis. Where are you? I'm picking you up."

"Do me and the world a favor. Go by yourself. Save condoms." I hang up.

One of Tupelo's landmarks rises in the distance—a water tower the city no longer uses that's shaped like a golf ball on a tee. I hang a left, then wheel into the parking lot beside the shotgun house where Elvis (the icon, not my dog) was born. It's two rooms with front and back doors aligned so you can shoot through the front and out the back.

Suddenly I'm out of steam. I just sit in the Dodge Ram gripping the steering wheel.

"That does it," Lovie says. "You're spending the night with me."

She rummages for her cell phone. This could take two weeks: she has a purse the size of Texas. I hand her mine and she calls Janice Laton.

"Callie won't be home tonight. I trust everybody can get along fine without her. . . . Great. Oh, if her basset hound shows up, give us a call."

She gives Janice both our numbers. "Let's get out of here, Callie. We need hot fudge."

It's getting too dark to see, anyway, and I've never known a problem that couldn't be made better with chocolate. I head back west in the gathering gloom. We nab her van at the funeral home, then end up on Robins Street.

You'd expect somebody Lovie's size to have a house like mine—ten-foot ceilings, big rooms, massive closets. She lives in a doll's house, a little pink cottage on a postage-stamp, magnolia studded lot a few blocks from the heart of downtown Tupelo. The only spacious room in her house is the kitchen.

She makes two hot fudge sundaes, then rifles through her CDs and selects Pachelbel's Canon in D. We sprawl on her blue velvet sofa with our feet on the coffee table, needing no communication except music and chocolate.

Lovie's penchant for highbrow music surprises most people.

When she was sixteen, she wanted to be a classical pianist. She's a genius at the keyboard and could easily have been a professional musician, but after Aunt Minrose choked to death on a chicken bone at the Sunday dinner table, Lovie gave up lofty aspirations in favor of ice cream and boys. But even so, she still looks like a plus-sized Rita Hayworth.

After dinner I borrow one of her one-size-fits-all nightshirts with a slogan that says *Hero Wanted, Apply Here,* and we settle in for a marathon of watching old cowboy movies.

"The great thing about westerns is that you can always tell the bad guys by their black hats." Lovie says this in a way that makes me wonder if she's just searching through all those men till she finds one with a white hat.

The thing is, Jack wears black all the time, but deep down if I thought that made him one of the really bad guys I wouldn't let him touch me with a ten-foot pole. Or any other size, for that matter. But that man has settled into my heart and no matter how hard I try, I can't get him out.

The miniature Big Ben on Lovie's TV chimes half past midnight. I head to bed while Lovie stays behind to watch *The Lone Ranger.*

"I never could resist a man in tight pants and a mask," she says.

She loves to leave you laughing.

● ● ●

Lovie's phone wakes me up at the crack of eight. In my opinion the day shouldn't start till ten o'clock. I luxuriate in my cousin's single bed. The tiny guest room has rose-sprigged wallpaper that makes me think of being in the middle of my gardens.

The phone keeps ringing.

"Lovie, do you want me to get that?"

I take her silence as either a yes or an indication that she's going deaf. I pick up the bedside phone and say, "Hello."

"Callie, is that you?" It's Uncle Charlie. "You and Lovie have to get over to the funeral home. Quick. Leonard Laton's gone."

"Where did he go?"

"Are you awake, dear heart? His body's missing."

After I roust Lovie out of bed, we climb into my Dodge Ram and hotfoot it to the funeral home.

The only other times I've seen Uncle Charlie this upset were when Aunt Minrose passed away and when he lost his favorite fishing pole in the Tennessee/Tombigbee Waterway.

"What happened?" I ask, and he leads us into the viewing room where we get a shocking view of Leonard Laton's empty casket. "Who would want to steal the doctor's body?"

"Not Janice or Mellie," Lovie says, "unless Janice

wants to leave him in a field for the vultures."

"Besides," I say, "neither one of them looks stout enough to tote a dead body. Unless they were in cahoots."

"Those two?" Lovie says. "If they were Siamese twins they'd try to live in different states."

"How do you know?" I ask.

"Yesterday before Janice stormed off in her rental car I overheard her telling Mellie she'd fly her lawyer out from California. Mellie said she'd eat arsenic before she'd trust anybody with an earring in the wrong ear."

"My question is how?" Uncle Charlie closes and locks the casket. "I have a security system. It would take an expert to crack it, but apparently that's what happened. There was no sign of forced entry."

"Uncle Charlie, what did Grover Grimsley say about Bevvie?"

"Nobody's seen her since last Tuesday when she left the Serengeti."

"Look on the bright side," I tell him. "Nobody knows when we can bury the doctor. And his children certainly aren't going to waste their time standing around viewing the body of a man who cut them out of his will."

"I've never lost a body. You and Lovie have to help me find it before anybody knows it's missing."

Good grief. Lovie can barely find her car keys

and I can't even find my dog. How does Uncle Charlie expect us to find a missing corpse? Still, I can't disappoint my favorite—and only—uncle.

Mama sweeps in looking like the empress of a small county in a purple tunic embroidered with gold and green dragons, black toreador pants, and cute wedge-heeled espadrilles I covet.

"You're late." Uncle Charlie kisses her on the cheek. "How are you, Ruby Nell?"

Richer, I'm hoping, but now is not the time and place to ask.

"How'd that old codger escape, Charlie? Knowing him, I thought he might have come back from the dead, but I didn't see any resurrected rakes driving a black Mercedes on Highway 78."

The four of us go into his office for a family summit. The gist of it all is that although the doctor's public viewing won't be held till Bevvie turns up, everybody in town who read the obituary knows he's dead and anybody could have done the dastardly deed. (Mama's term for the body snatching.)

The bottom line: Lovie and I will search for the wandering corpse while Mama and Uncle Charlie stall the Latons on the remote chance any of them will find the milk of human forgiveness in their souls (another of Mama's terms) and want to see their dead daddy.

"Daddy, we can't just go barging around town asking if anybody's seen a corpse."

"Go about your ordinary business, Lovie. Between you and Callie, you see just about everybody in Lee County on a daily basis. And, sweetheart, be discreet."

He might as well tell a brass band to tone down.

In the parking lot, Lovie and I devise a plan.

"What are we going to do first, Lovie?"

"Eat cake. My house."

Back in her glorious rose-colored kitchen with the shiny green-tiled countertops, she heats a frozen cinnamon/pecan coffee cake and pours rich Colombian coffee into two china cups.

"I wonder if the doctor had enemies?" I dig into the coffee cake.

"What doctor doesn't? I'd like to kill mine every time he does a pap smear."

"Any one of his disgruntled patients could have stolen him. This is depressing."

"Have another piece of cake."

"Maybe we ought to start with the obvious suspect."

"Who would that be, Callie?"

"Bubbles Malone. One, she's the wild card in this Laton farce, and two, she's big enough to move the body."

"Don't forget three. She inherited all the money. She and the doctor had to be tight."

"My point, exactly," I tell Lovie.

"But why would she want a corpse? And how in

the heck would she get it home, wherever that is?"

"Maybe she didn't fly in. Maybe she drove. Anyhow, we don't have to figure out why. Or even how. Just who."

"Got any bright ideas, Sherlock?"

"We could just march up and ask Grover where she lives, but he'd never betray attorney/client privilege. And if he would, I wouldn't have him for a lawyer. Besides, he might have contacted her through her lawyer."

"Maybe I can pump the information out of him."

I swat her with my napkin. "I'll put Bubbles' name on the beauty parlor grapevine while you check out all the motels."

"Been there, done that."

"Smart aleck. Let's just see if we can find her."

"Then what? Tie her to a tree with my bra and torture her with hot fudge till she confesses?"

"I'll think of something."

After I leave Lovie's I barely have time to whiz by my house to check on the California Latons, feed the menagerie of homeless pets I'm trying to decide whether to keep, and see if Elvis is back. As I dump cat food into seven separate dishes and feed the bottomless pit cocker spaniel, I figure that if I keep rescuing stray animals my pet food bill will exceed my mortgage.

Elvis is still missing, much to my dismay, and the Laton gang is nowhere to be found, much to my wicked glee. I briefly consider calling Jack for a missing dog bulletin, but I'm in no mood to bite off more than I can chew, so I change clothes and head to Hair.Net.

My first customer is already there, waiting outside in the 1967 funeral hearse she bought and converted to her personal limousine by painting it neon green with *Gas, Grits, and Guts* in hot pink on the side.

We go inside and I set about mixing the strong ammonia solution for Fayrene's permanent wave.

The last time I did a perm Elvis deliberately found a dried-up, flattened frog and left it on my front porch with the morning paper.

I start rolling Fayrene's hair in tissue paper and random-sized rods, and casually drop Bubbles Malone into the beauty parlor grapevine.

"She came by the store yesterday," Fayrene says, then proceeds to give me a blow-by-blow account.

The minute she leaves I rush to my office to call Lovie. All I get is her voice mail.

"Lovie, call me the minute you get this message."

My next appointment is not till three o'clock, so I call to see if Mama is back from the funeral home.

When I lock up, it's starting to rain. Elvis hates getting wet. Wherever he is, I hope he's found a dry spot.

By the time I get to the farm, it's pouring.

My hair's the good, thick straight kind I could put through a typhoon and it would still fall back into place. I don't have to worry about makeup, either. With my brown eyes and olive skin I could go without a smidge and you'd hardly notice. It's my Juicy Couture sandals with the turquoise and rhinestone straps I'm worried about.

I kick them off in the truck, then race into Mama's brick bungalow barefoot.

"I doubled your money." Mama hands me a towel to dry off. "But the roulette wheel double-crossed me."

"Which means you lost my money."

"Well, not all of it."

She fishes in her purse and hands me ten dollars, which I won't even dignify with a comment. Instead I tell her about Elvis' disappearance.

"I thought I saw him a little while ago," she says. "I went out back to pick some fresh basil for soup and I thought that was Elvis and another dog streaking across the pasture."

I jump up and rummage in Mama's closet till I find her raincoat and boots.

"Where are you going?"

"To see if that was my dog."

"You'll catch cold and die of double pneumonia, and I don't even have any more Italian marble monuments."

"Good grief, Mama."

Thank goodness the rain has slacked. I slosh

across the pasture yelling, "Elvis. Come here, boy."

"He ain't here."

Holy cow! At first I think I'm looking at an apparition, and then I realize it's a strange man wearing a black slicker and rain hat and carrying a fishing pole. He looks shady to me.

I'm torn between running and asking how he knows my dog. Elvis wins.

"You've seen Elvis?" I ask.

"No, but my wife did. Over at the Piggly Wiggly in Fulton. She said he'd lost about fifty pounds and was wearing one of them tight blue suits with all them rhinestones on it. Of course, you might not want to believe her. She's gone mental."

Maybe he has, too, and maybe I'm fixing to stand here and get my throat cut. What's he doing in Mama's pasture, anyhow?

"You're on Valentine property."

"Yep, I knew your daddy. He used to let me come here all the time. I guess you don't remember."

He's right about that. But I do remember that Daddy would never say no when a stranger showed up on the farm with his fishing pole and a yen to try for the catfish bottom-feeding in our two-acre lake.

"You're fishing?"

"Yep. Fish bite in weather like this. Hope you don't mind. Name's Buck Witherspoon."

53

"You'd better take that up with Uncle Charlie. Charles Sebastian Valentine. He's listed in the phone book."

When he leaves I make a mental note to ask Uncle Charlie about him. I believe in fate, not coincidence. You never can tell who might want to steal a body. Maybe he's checking to see what else he can steal from the Valentines.

Mama would call my encounter in the pasture a brush with death, but I'm not about to tell her and give her one more reason to tell me I should go back to Jack Jones.

"For protection," she'd say. I know her like a book.

She has hot soup and corn bread waiting, and we have a late lunch before I head back to the beauty parlor. On the way, my cell phone rings.

"I have news," Lovie says. "Bubbles Malone checked into the Holiday Inn."

"Great."

"Not so great. She's checked out. There's no telling where she is now."

"Las Vegas." I tell her about Fayrene's Bubble sighting at Gas, Grits, and Guts. "Fayrene even remembers the car she was driving. A ninety-eight Honda hatchback. With Nevada license plates."

"That still doesn't mean she's on the lam with a stolen corpse."

"I know, but why did she leave Tupelo in such a hurry? If she was close enough to inherit all his money, wouldn't you think she'd want to stick around for the funeral?"

"Yeah, unless she's afraid one of the disinherited will do her in. And how would she get a stiff in that little bitty car?"

Good grief. Now that we're part-time sleuths (more or less), Lovie's started talking like Humphrey Bogart doing film noir.

"Lovie, she's the only lead we have."

"I guess that means we're taking a road trip out West."

"Don't mention Las Vegas to Mama or she'll want to go. I can't afford for her to lose another spin of the roulette wheel."

"I'm very good at creative truth."

Of course, this means I'm fixing to have to tell a few lies, myself, because how I can go off on a road trip when I have a house full of Latons who don't know their daddy's missing, a missing dog who thinks he's a rock 'n' roll legend, and an almost-ex who's just itching for me to prove myself an unfit pet mother?

Chapter 4

Big City, Big Lies, Big Trouble

Expert sleuths would probably jump into their car and tail Bubbles across the Painted Desert, but Lovie and I are real women with business obligations and real lives (sort of). We have to make plans before we can leave town.

When I leave the beauty parlor I make another circuit of the neighborhood hoping to spot Elvis. No luck. I drag myself home in the rain feeling lower than a fattening hog on butchering day.

The Laton crew is not back at my house, but Jack Jones is. Sitting on my front porch swing bigger than sin. I can't say, "Get off my property," because he still owns it.

"Callie, I'm leaving town."

"As if I want to know. Permanently, I hope."

"You never could lie."

"That's not a lie. It's wishful thinking."

I don't tell him I'm leaving town, too. It's none of his business.

"I'll be in the Black Hills."

"Panning for gold?"

"Cute, Callie."

All six delicious feet of him unfolds and I prime myself to be backed against the porch railing and seduced in plain view of the neighbors. Instead he rakes me close, gives me a black-eyed stare that nearly sets my hair on fire, then turns me loose so fast I don't know whether I've been almost ravished or run over by a freight train.

"If I get started, I won't stop." He strides to his silver Jag and roars off into the sunset. Or what would be the sunset if it weren't still raining cats and dogs.

Every dog, that is, except Elvis.

After I get my galloping libido under control and stick another Band-Aid on my patched-up heart, I take care of my temporary cats and short-term dog. (I only started collecting strays a year ago when Jack left, and I wonder what that tells me about myself.) Afterward I eat a pimento sandwich standing up, then go into my bedroom to decide what I'm going to take to Las Vegas.

Seized by sudden inspiration, I go into the guest bedroom and search through the Latons' luggage. I don't know what I expect to find. Daddy Laton stuffed in the Luis Vuitton?

If Janice catches me, I wonder if she can accuse me of trespassing and have me thrown in jail. Is it trespassing if you're in your own house?

My cell phone rings and I nearly jump through the ceiling.

"You sound funny," Lovie says. "What are you up to?"

"I'm up to my elbows in Janice Laton's Victoria's Secret underwear."

"Is there something you haven't told me?"

"Good grief, Lovie. I'm searching for clues."

"Find anything?"

"I found out she wears size six."

"Bikinis or full cut?"

"Full cut."

"It figures. Listen, Callie, we'd better take my van so we'll have a place to put the body."

"It'll fit in the back of my Dodge Ram." I hate the way Lovie drives. As if every highway is the Talladega Speedway. "We'll cover it with a tarp."

"If we get caught in the middle of a summer hailstorm we'll be hauling the doctor back in pieces. Besides, if we don't tie him down right he's liable to blow out somewhere in the desert and we'd never find him."

A few days ago the most exciting thing in my life was finding Ferragamo shoes on sale. Now I'm discussing the best way to haul a corpse across a desert.

"All right, Lovie. We'll take your van."

"Good. I'll pick you up after lunch tomorrow. I'm catering a bridesmaid's brunch in the morning."

"That works. I have to reschedule my appointments, talk to Mama about staying up here so the Latons won't tear down my house, and see my lawyer."

"About what?"

"I want to talk to him about taking out an ad to find Elvis."

• • •

"Absolutely not," Grover Grimsley says.

It's 10:00 A.M., and I'm sitting in his office bleary-eyed from dreaming about being chased across the desert by corpses, while Janice and crew are sleeping off their ill tempers in my upstairs guest bedrooms. I didn't hear them come in till one o'clock this morning.

"Why not?" I ask Grover. "I'm desperate to find Elvis."

"It's bad enough you called Jack and he knows Elvis vanished under your care. Still, it's your word against his. An ad would provide him written proof you're an unfit pet mother."

"I am not."

"I'm only playing devil's advocate, Callie."

He's so good at being the devil he scared me. Now if he can just scare Jack Jones into signing divorce papers, I'll be a free woman. Then I can celebrate. Or cry, which seems more likely at the moment.

"Have you found Bevvie Laton yet?" I ask.

"No. Apparently she's left Africa. I hate to tell Charlie, but it looks as if the funeral's on hold indefinitely."

"I'll tell him. I'm going over to the funeral home."

When I get there, Mama's on the second floor of Eternal Rest with Uncle Charlie, which is where he lives. Personally I think he'd be better off some-

59

where that didn't have the deceased waiting around downstairs for their send-off to the here-after, but that's just me. I'd hate to think I couldn't walk out of my house without having to pass through a fog of hair spray, styling mousse, and perm fumes.

It's bad enough just being a celebrity. I can't walk into Gas, Grits, and Guts without having somebody walk over and consult me about color and shampoo.

I walk in and sit on Uncle Charlie's brown leather sofa in front of a wall of books that would be the envy of the Lee County Library.

"I was about to drown tromping around the monuments," Mama says, "so I shut down for the day and brought Charlie some leftover soup."

She's in tangerine today. Head to toe. It's not her color, but I'm not about to tell her. She doesn't take criticism well, even when it's constructive. Unless Uncle Charlie's the one delivering it.

"If it weren't for me," she adds, "Charlie would eat nothing but peanut butter and crackers."

Uncle Charlie winks at me. We both know this is not true. He's a better cook than Mama, but he lets her feed him anyway because he knows she likes to be needed. He's the one who told her not to sell the monument business after Daddy died because he knew she needed something to do.

"But, Charlie," she told him. "I don't know beans about running a business."

"You'll catch on, Ruby Nell," he told her, and she did. It took her two years, and he was at her side every time she had a question.

Uncle Charlie is the rock of this family, always fixing what's wrong. It feels good to be the one to deliver good news about the lead on the missing body and the lack of leads on Bevvie's whereabouts.

"The bad news is, I'll need Mama to stay with my houseguests and I haven't found Elvis yet."

"How long will I be in prison?" Trust Mama to put herself at the center.

"At least a week."

That counts driving time to and from Vegas because we certainly don't want to declare a missing corpse on an airplane. I keep this information to myself. If Mama got wind of our destination, she'd insist on going and we'd never get home. I'd have to become hairdresser to the stars.

I wonder if Wayne Newton is still alive. He could use a new hairdo.

"Don't worry, dear heart. You find the body. Ruby Nell and I will find your dog."

"You might want to ask Jack to go along on your trip, Callie," Mama says.

"Why?"

"You might need his gun. Among other things."

"This is just a missing corpse case, Mama, not murder."

When I leave and Uncle Charlie walks me to my

Dodge Ram, I tell him about seeing Buck Witherspoon on the farm.

"Don't worry, dear heart. I'll take care of him."

Goodness gracious. That sounds clandestine to me. And slightly dangerous. I wouldn't want to be in this Witherspoon character's shoes.

When Uncle Charlie hugs me, he slips a wad of cash into my pocket. "For the trip. If you need more, let me know. You and Lovie be careful, dear heart."

Does my uncle know something he's not telling me? Maybe I ought to rethink Jack and his smoking pistol.

Armed with our suitcases and two cans of pepper spray (my idea, though I don't know who I expect to use it on) plus a hamper filled with Diet Pepsis and enough junk food to feed a third world country (Lovie's idea), we strike out at the stroke of one with the full intention of driving straight through to Vegas. We figure we can make it in thirty-four hours if we take turns behind the wheel.

Good intentions bite the dust in Albuquerque, New Mexico. We hole up in a Comfort Inn for a few hours, then hit the road at the crack of nine thirty the next morning.

In the middle of the night we drag into Vegas, pumped on caffeine and ready to take the city by storm. Vegas is a night city. Lights ablaze.

Crowds thronging the casinos. Party-till-you-drop atmosphere.

We check into a cheap, no-tell motel on the edge of the Strip, and Lovie sprawls on the bed while I grab the phone book and start checking under the *M*s.

"Good grief, Callie. What are you going to do if you find her? We can't barge over there in the middle of the night."

"I just want to see if she's listed, that's all. She has a head start. We can't afford to dally." I trace my finger down the list of *M*s. "Shoot. She's unlisted. We have work to do. Let's go get 'em, tiger."

We shuck our shorts for killer outfits, hail a cab (we're both too tired to drive), then head into the city that never sleeps. Lovie looks like a firestorm in a flashy red sequined dress and rhinestone earrings as big as Arkansas, and I look about ten feet tall in a brand-new pair of stiletto-heeled, lizard-skin Enzo Angiolini sling-backs.

At Caesars Palace where Bubbles last worked, we split up at the roulette wheel and agree to meet there in two hours. I look across the sea of people and see nothing but bad haircuts and split ends.

If I'm ever going to find Dr. Laton's corpse I've got to quit thinking like a hairstylist and start thinking like Humphrey Bogart doing Phillip Marlowe.

I pick out a distinguished-looking gray-haired couple who would have been old enough to afford show tickets around the time Bubbles was probably in her performing prime. Translation: before she started needing a forklift to hold up her breasts.

I head their way and prepare to exaggerate my drawl. A southern accent is a good ice breaker if you're outside the Deep South.

"Hello, I wonder (pronounced *wonnndah)* if you nice folks could help me *(he'p meee)."*

They stare at me as if I've landed from another planet and plan to start eating senior citizens first.

"I'm *(ahhh'm)* from a little ole fan club in Dallas called FTS—that's Find the Stars—and I was hoping I'd *(ahhh'd)* find somebody who might know one of my favorites. Bubbles Malone."

"What'd she say, Gertrude?"

Pointing to his ear, Gertrude yells, "Turn on your hearing aide, Hubert." Hubert complies, then winces when she yells, "She's from the PTO and wants to know about somebody named Bubble Along."

He taps me on the shoulder. Hard. "Young lady, I'm from the MYOB club. That's mind your own business."

They turn and walk in the opposite direction, but not before he shoots me the bird.

"That didn't go so well."

"What didn't go well?"

I nearly jump through the gaudy two-ton chandelier. If it fell on somebody, it'd kill them.

Lovie has sneaked up behind me, apparently determined to cause my first gray hair.

"Where'd you come from?"

"Two proposals and six indecent propositions. Let's get out of here. My butt's black and blue from unsolicited pinchings."

"Okay. Maybe we'll have better luck at the MGM Grand."

We weave our way through the crowd and onto the Strip to hail a cab. There we are, minding our own business (almost), when a young man in torn jeans and a dirty muscle shirt streaks by and grabs my purse.

"What next?" I say.

"We catch his skinny carcass and beat the daylights out of him. Come on."

Lovie steamrolls down the street with me barreling along right beside her. I'd hate to be in our path.

Elvis' Opinion # 3 on the Southern Mafia, Rocket Science, and Garbage Cans

My plan was to take a few days off to get to know my little French sweetie, show her the sights, then head on home and introduce her to my human mom.

You know what they say about the best-laid plans of mice and men, and I reckon that includes basset hounds. Callie's not home.

For one thing, Ruby Nell has moved into our house. That would never happen unless (a) one of them is sick or dying or (b) Callie's gone. Not that they don't get along. They do. You just can't coop two strong-willed women up together for more than twenty-four hours and expect peace in the valley.

For another, I can smell Callie a mile.

She smells like a flower. Gardenia. And it's not perfume, either. She has a natural set of powerful pheromones that roped in my human daddy and made him forget he'd planned on being a bachelor till the day he died. Which could be sooner than later. You ought to see his arsenal. Knives, guns, rifles, machetes. He's got 'em all, and he knows how to use them, too.

Of course, he's an expert at keeping secrets. The only weapon Callie knows about is the Colt .45.

And I'll never tell the rest. She's got enough on her mind keeping up with the Valentines and the Latons' dirty laundry.

And I'm not talking blue jeans.

Just because I'm taking a little R and R, don't think I don't know what's going on. Finding stuff out's not rocket science if you know the fine points of eavesdropping.

Yesterday when I was on the farm showing Ann Margret around (well, bragging, if you want to know the truth), I overheard Ruby Nell and Charlie talking about the body snatching. (Obviously, they'd met down there to talk about things they didn't want the Latons to know.)

If they had put me on the job, they'd never have lost the body in the first place. But what can I say? Don't step on my blue suede shoes? Everybody in the world loved me when I was crooning gold and giving away Cadillacs, but Callie's the only one of the Valentines with a true appreciation of my talents.

Of course, if they'd put me on the job I wouldn't have met my little French poodle. Don't get me wrong. I'm not one to get my head turned by every Raquel rottweiler and Shelley sheepdog that walks by. But let a honey like Ann Margret come along and a basset hound can't help falling in love.

But even fools have to eat.

I sashay over to the garbage can behind the truck stop to see what's cooking. Coleslaw. Cabbage.

Dill pickles. It might do for stray cats but not for a King.

I head down to the farm with Ann Margret trotting along beside me to see what I can find in Ruby Nell's garbage cans. Day-old meat loaf, half a loaf of Wonder bread, a big hunk of lemon pound cake. The woman's a kindred spirit. I wonder if she was a basset hound in another life.

After lunch Ann Margret and I take a dip in the lake and are just vegging out under the oak tree when this sleazy-looking character I've never seen shows up with his rod and reel. If you ask me, something fishy's going on, and it's not catfish.

If I were a Doberman I'd haul off across the pasture and take a bite out of his leg, but I'm nonviolent by nature. I prefer to sit back and see if we can settle our differences by peaceful means.

The stranger meanders around the east side of the lake, looks over his shoulder, then heads toward Ruby Nell's house.

"Take another step in that direction and you'll wish you hadn't, Buck."

I can smell Buck's fear all the way over here. Obviously he didn't see Charlie Valentine coming and neither did I. Maybe the rumors about Charlie are true: a man who can move with that kind of stealth just might be mixed up with the Southern Mafia.

"I was fishing. Your brother said I could."

"He didn't know what I know. I'm making you

an offer you can't refuse. You can leave politely and never come near Ruby Nell again or I'll help you pack and escort you to the state line. You don't want to have to do that again, do you, Buck?"

Apparently there's a long history between these two, and I plan to find out about it. But not today.

Charlie watches Buck scuttle back toward his truck, while I take advantage of the diversion to vanish into the woods with my sweet Frenchie. If Charlie sees me, he'll insist I go home, and I've still got a lot of business to take care of.

Elvis has left the building, baby.

Chapter 5

Hot Tips, Hair Spray, and Undercover Bombshells

S top, you little troglodyte."

Lovie's yelling at the twerp who stole my purse, while I huff along in her wake trying to catch up. You'd think somebody with my long legs couldn't be outrun by a person three inches shorter and seventy pounds heavier.

"I don't think he knows what troglodyte means, Lovie."

I'm panting and there's a stitch in my side I'm sure will turn into a ruptured major organ any minute.

"When I catch you I'm going to relocate your ears," she screams right before she pounces.

Both of them go down like felled redwoods. By the time I get there, Lovie's sitting on the petty thief with her legs crossed. He's flattened like a frog and fighting for breath.

She tosses my purse to me. "What do you want me to do with this little pipsqueak, Callie?"

"Why don't we start by pulling his fingernails off?"

"Are you broads crazy? Get off me."

Lovie bounces a time or two, and you can hear his scream all the way to Mississippi.

"I think that's too tame," she says. "I think we ought to break both his knees."

"You already did, you big tub of lard."

She boxes both his ears. "Watch your mouth. You ought to be ashamed, talking to your elders like that. Maybe we ought to teach him some manners. What do you say, Callie?"

"We could tie him to the back of your van and drag him along the Strip. It needs a good cleaning."

"Call the cops," he begs. "Please, just call the cops."

Tears are streaming down his face. I almost feel sorry for him, but Lovie shows no mercy. She pats his backside.

"Have a seat, Callie. Let's think about this awhile."

I shift trying to get some relief from the stitch in my side and he yells, "Sweet Jesus!"

Lovie winks at me and I pull out my cell phone and give him a reprieve. It takes three of the LVPD to get Lovie up. While one of the officers takes my statement and another cuffs the repentant thief, Lovie asks the third, a fresh-faced young man with red freckles, about Bubbles Malone. Officer Jenkins, according to his badge.

"She was an exotic dancer, I think," Lovie says. "Probably about twenty-five or thirty years ago."

"No. I've never heard of her."

That doesn't surprise me. I have tennis shoes

older than this man. But no matter what their age, they all fall victim to Lovie's charm.

"You've just pulled out a thorn in the backside of Vegas," Jenkins tells her. "We've been trying to catch this perp for six weeks. You wouldn't be looking for a job, would you?"

"You never can tell."

Flirting is second nature to Lovie. If I don't get her out of here, she'll be making a date and teaching Jenkins a few new tricks.

He hails us a cab, but we're too tired to continue our search so we head back to our motel, where we compare notes while Lovie rubs Ben Gay on her hips and I put Band-Aids on my blistered heels. Yellow with smiley faces. What can I say? I'm a woman of simple pleasures.

"Are you okay, Lovie?"

"I'm fine." She rubs Bengay on her thighs, too. "I should have used pepper spray on that little turd."

I inspect my feet for more damage. "Fayrene's been wanting some Enzo Angiolinis. I'm giving these to her as soon as I get home."

One of the reasons I'm so popular in Mooreville is that my customers eventually get my designer shoes, sometimes after they've been worn only once.

"This is not working, Callie."

"What?"

"Just going around asking questions. The minute

73

I open my mouth the locals clam up as if I'm fixing to turn them in for lobbying against Christmas."

She's right. At the rate we're going, we'll never find Bubbles, let alone the doctor's body. There's only one thing to do.

"Lovie, we're going undercover. And don't you dare say, been there, done that."

"Okay, I won't. What's plan B?"

"I can get backstage as a hairdresser and makeup artist. You can be my assistant."

"No, I've always wanted to be a star. I'll pose as a showgirl."

The thought boggles my mind.

She hefts herself off the bed and strikes a come-hither pose and I hit her with a pillow. She tosses it back and we fall into bed.

I'm lying under my sheets dreaming I'm a slot machine and Jack's just hit triple cherries when my cell phone jars me awake. I scramble for it in the dark, then punch the Talk button while I head toward the bathroom so I won't wake Lovie. Sitting on the side of the cold porcelain tub with my bare feet on the even colder tile floor, I whisper, "Hello."

It's Jack. "I hear you're in Las Vegas looking for some missing goods."

"How did you know?"

"I have my ways."

One of his ways happens to be melting my bones every time I hear his voice. It's a deep, sexy rumble you'd expect from a man who, without his clothes, looks like he ought to be doing triple-X-rated movies. Also, even with his clothes.

"I'm hanging up now, Jack."

"Don't you want to know where I am?"

"No."

"Close enough to pull your cute buns out of the fire. Call me if you need me, babe."

"Don't hold your breath."

Where Jack's concerned I can't even come up with a retort that's not cliché. If I knew a way to cure myself of him, I would. I've burned white candles under the full moon, consulted a psychic, and even tried to get on *Dr. Phil.* But Jack's like Staph in the heart, an infection that just won't go away.

I tiptoe out of the bathroom, which turns out to be an unnecessary precaution. The way Lovie's snoring it will take a Judgment Day trumpet call to wake her up. I get into bed and pull up the covers, but my feet are freezing, so I have to get back out again and rummage around in my suitcase looking for socks.

That man's more trouble than he's worth. Of course, there was a time Jack was the first person I ran to with my problems. He had a knack for fixing things and making it look easy while *not* making me feel like a fool for asking.

If I keep following this train of thought, I'll get derailed and start second-guessing myself about the divorce. I'm not going to think about that tonight. I'm going to be Scarlett O'Hara and think about it tomorrow.

Or whenever we find Dr. Laton and get him back in his casket at Eternal Rest.

I fall into bed and pray for a dreamless sleep, or at least one that does not feature my almost-ex winning my jackpot.

Going undercover is not as easy as it sounds.

First we have to find a casino that will believe Lovie as a hundred-and-ninety-pound bombshell, over-the-hill showgirl.

After spending the morning checking every run-down casino on the Strip we finally end up at our last hope—Hot Tips, a ramshackle club on the fringes that looks as if it saw its best days during the reign of Bugsy Seagal.

The owner—a swarthy man smoking a cigar bigger than he is—has no trouble picturing me as hairdresser and makeup artist to the stars. But when Lovie plops the "showgirl wanted" ad in front of him, he nearly swallows his cigar.

"What are your credentials?"

"Les Follies Bergere, Paris. In France I'm a national treasure."

I knew Lovie had a talent for fiction, but I never knew she could lie with such a straight face.

"Show me what you've got," he says.

"If I show you everything I've got, you won't survive it."

"You're hired. Go backstage and let wardrobe find you a costume that fits."

"That'll be a miracle on the order of the parting of the Red Sea," she tells me as we wind our way through darkened hallways that make me want to whip out my cell phone and dial 911.

Finally we find wardrobe behind a plywood door with faded gold lettering. Lovie goes through a pair of gray curtains while I wait in a small, spare sitting area in an uncomfortable straight-backed chair. I'm flipping through an out-of-date fashion magazine as if I have a burning interest in hair-styles from 1996 when she bursts through the curtains.

"Don't you dare laugh," she says, and then we both crack up. In full regalia, complete with a ten-foot-tall feathered headdress, she looks like a molting Big Bird.

"I'm showing more skin than the Goodyear Blimp. Why don't we skip plan B and go straight to plan C?"

"Which is?"

"Something that doesn't feature me in feathers. I'm itching."

"That's why God made Benadryl."

We have time for a quick supper and a phone call to Mississippi before we head out for our under-cover performances. I call Uncle Charlie, partially because he's more likely to give a coherent report from the home front, but mostly because I'm afraid Mama will find us on her slot machine radar and catch the next plane west.

"I haven't seen a sign of Elvis, dear heart," he tells me. "But Ruby Nell and I are still looking."

"By any chance, has the corpse reappeared?"

I ask this question while crossing my fingers behind my back and making a silent devil-at-the-crossroads promise to give up cute shoes. But only the ones with big price tags.

"No. But at least the Latons haven't asked to see the body. What about Leonard Laton?"

"The lead's still hot," I say, and Lovie rolls her eyes.

"Well, it is," I tell her after I hang up. "We're going to find the body. Are you ready?"

"Ready for what? My ass looks like the moon over Miami."

"Well, all right, then. Let's get out there and shine."

Armed with enough glitter hair spray and Cover Girl makeup to paint another desert, we head to Hot Tips.

The parking lot is full and the casino/nightclub is packed. Their public appeal has to be the cheapest drinks in town and the low cover charge, because one quick look backstage tells me these showgirls are mostly has-beens and rejects from the bigger, classier clubs in the heart of the Strip.

Beside them, Lovie looks like a star. I'm glad. I'd hate to have to beat somebody up. But if anybody insults her or makes a wrong move in her direction or even looks at her sideways, I'll whip off my pink Fendis and smack them with the four-inch heel. I swear to Neiman Marcus.

I leave Lovie getting acquainted with the other showgirls while I spread my makeup at a dressing table under a long bank of lighted mirrors.

"You new here?"

I say yes, and the long-legged exotic dancer plops into my chair.

"See what you can do with this face." She has grooves deeper than the Grand Canyon, but I'm up to the challenge. "I'm Candi with an *i*."

"Nancy," I say, and start sponging on medium bronze pancake.

When you're involved in skullduggery, you never know when somebody with a big gun is going to come after you. I smooth a darker shade to define Candi's cheekbones.

"Say, you're really good. Have you been at this long?"

"Long enough to wish I could have worked on some of the really big Vegas stars. Like Bubbles Malone. Have you ever heard of her?"

"That name rings a bell. Wait a minute." She twists around in her chair. "Hey, Divine, come over here a minute."

A woman with sleek skin as dark as a panther's

glides over. Although I stand six feet in four-inch heels, I'm dwarfed by her.

"Do you remember a dancer named Bubbles?" Candi asks. "Bubbles Malone?"

"Yeah. But she wasn't Malone back then. She was Bubbles Daily."

"She was my personal hero," I say. "I'd just love to meet her. Do you happen to know where she lives?"

"Sure. You got anything to write on?"

Divine scrawls the address in eyebrow pencil on a napkin from Hot Tips, then races to line up for her performance. I'll have to wait until after the show to tell Lovie.

The houselights go down, and I go up front and grope for an empty seat. Finally I find one beside a man the size of a Whirlpool refrigerator.

The drums roll, the curtains part, and I sit back to watch the moon rise over Miami.

Chapter 6

Lemonade, Pregnant Cats, and Frozen Stiffs

Armed with a map of Las Vegas and a half-baked plan, we set out at the crack of ten the next morning to pay a social call on Bubbles Malone. Lovie's driving and I'm navigating. Or trying to. Reading maps is not my strong point.

In a subdivision on the outskirts of town where

all the houses look alike and the street names are hidden on little posts the size of toothpicks, I spot a blood-red Ford pickup behind us. The driver is a hulking stranger with a baseball cap pulled low over his eyes.

"Somebody's following us, Lovie."

"How do you know?"

"He's up your tailpipe. And that driver looks like he knows how to use a machine gun."

She glances in the rearview mirror. "I think it's my secret admirer from Hot Tips."

"Who?"

"How do I know? I had so many I couldn't keep their names straight."

"Good grief."

"Besides, if it's the one I'm thinking, he never did come close enough to introduce himself. I think he's shy."

"Then how do you know he's an admirer?"

"I can smell lust a mile." She whips onto Cactus Street—Bubbles' current address if my information is correct—and the Ford truck keeps on going. "See, I told you. He's shy."

"Driving a bad-ass Ford F-150 four-by-four with a roll bar and enough lights on top to spotlight every snake in the Painted Desert? I don't think so."

"You're losing it, Callie."

She pulls into the driveway of 106 Cactus, and parks behind a '98 Honda hatchback.

"I am *not*. But you do the talking, Lovie. I'll conduct the search." She excels at fiction. She'd have to, to keep so many men on the string.

Lovie and I bail out of the van, priss right up to the front door, and ring the bell. Elvis' mama and the national treasure of France back down at nothing.

After five rings, the door swings open. It's hard to recognize Bubbles without six inches of pancake makeup. Her red-rimmed eyes match a red chenille housecoat with most of the chenille rubbed off.

"What a surprise." She fiddles with the collar of her housecoat.

"Hi, Ms. Malone. We're the Valentine cousins from Tupelo. Remember us?" Lovie dazzles her with a smile that ought to be bottled and used for world peace. "Callie and I drove west for a little vacation, and we thought we'd drop by to see how you're doing." Lovie reaches for her hand. "I know losing the doctor had to be hard for you. Are you okay?"

"I'm flattered. Come on in." Bubbles swings open the door and Lovie gives me the high five behind her back. "Excuse the mess. I'm getting ready to do a little redecorating."

The inside of her house looks like a yard sale. Rattan furniture vies for floor space with Early American maple, magazines overflow their baskets, and every conceivable inch of wall space is covered with cheap prints and doodads on what-not shelves.

She could hide a body in here and it would take a trained police dog seven weeks to find it.

"Sit down. I was just having a spot of lemonade. I'll get you some."

She heads toward the back, then returns with a huge pitcher of lemonade that explains her red-rimmed eyes. It's laced with so much alcohol, one sip nearly knocks me off the couch.

"Um, good," Lovie says. "Vodka?"

"Just a touch."

The two of them are going to get along like a house on fire.

"It's too bad you couldn't stay for the funeral," Lovie says.

"My cat's pregnant. I had to get home." Bubbles pours herself another glass and takes a slug. "It's a shame the family insisted on a regular funeral. Leonard wanted to be cremated and his ashes scattered in the Valley of Fire."

Holy cow. What if she's already cremated him? I picture Lovie and me combing the entire Valley of Fire, gathering Daddy Laton's ashes in a Wal-Mart bag.

"Have you known the doctor long?" I ask.

"Since I was eighteen. He was doctor to the showgirls when I was performing."

Lovie gives me a signal, so I ask for directions to the bathroom and leave her to handle the inquisition. I have some snooping to do.

I'll have to admit, I'm good at this. When Jack kept vanishing to parts unknown on business he refused to talk about, I started searching for clues to his secret life. The only thing I ever turned up was a plane ticket stub to Brazil, which explained exactly nothing. Still, if I'd kept at it, there's no telling what I'd have uncovered. But my conscience got the best of me. I was brought up to believe trust is the cornerstone of character and anything less is a crime, so I gave up stealth and settled into worry.

Now here I am, in the middle of Bubbles' bathroom, back in a life of crime. It's either leave Uncle Charlie in the lurch or live with a flawed character. Maybe after I find the corpse, I can reform.

A bathtub is an ideal fit for a stolen body, but one quick look behind the shower curtain tells me Bubbles is more creative than that. I sneak down the hall and into the kitchen, then freeze when I see her cat. Animals love me. It'll be just like that big gray Persian to leap off the table and race toward me, meowing with delight.

"Nice kitty," I whisper, then make a beeline for Bubbles' pantry. There's nothing in here except peaches and pickles.

I tiptoe out and through a door that leads to the utility room. Washer, dryer, clothes rack . . . and the perfect place to stash a body. A chest freezer.

As I inch that way, I hope the sweat running down my legs doesn't ruin my Steve Madden sandals. Sweat stains on leather are tacky.

I ease open the freezer, and hit pay dirt. If that's not Dr. Laton under the black tarp, then it's the biggest side of beef I've ever seen.

You wouldn't think I'd be squeamish peeling back the tarp to make sure, but let me tell you, applying pancake to a nice corpse who's planning to stay put in the friendly environs of Eternal Rest is entirely different from coming face-to-face with a frozen stiff with frostbite on his nose.

I ease the lid shut and stand there doing deep breathing till I can get enough starch back in my legs to walk to the living room.

"Is everything all right, hon?" Bubbles looks up when I enter the room. She also looks about three sheets to the wind. Thank goodness.

"I must be coming down with something." I rub my stomach and grimace.

"We'd better get you out of here." Lovie makes hasty good-byes to Bubbles, then grabs my arm and practically drags me out the door.

Bubbles stands in her front door waving while we back out of her driveway. In spite of the anxiety she's caused Uncle Charlie, I feel sorry for her. There are only two motives powerful enough to make a woman steal the body of a man who wanted his ashes scattered in the Valley of Fire.

Love or revenge. Soft touch that I am, I'm betting on love.

"Well?" Lovie says.

"I found him. In the freezer. Uncle Charlie is going to be relieved."

"We won't tell him yet."

"Why?"

"Because we've got to get him back, first. And that involves breaking and entering, stealing, and transporting an illegal corpse across state lines."

"That ought to be a cinch for a Mississippi caterer who showed half of Las Vegas the moon over Miami."

"At least stealing a body doesn't involve feathers. I'm hungry. Where do you want to eat?"

"The next restaurant you come to."

It turns out to be Chinese—not my favorite—but I can overlook MSG in the moo goo gai pan in exchange for relaxing in a little red vinyl booth with Christmas lights strung around the hanging lantern while I listen to Lovie's take on Bubbles' relationship with Dr. Laton.

"He was married when Bubbles knew him, but she doesn't strike me as the kind of woman who'd let a legal document stop her."

"He's old enough to be her daddy."

"So?"

I'm not going to touch that with a ten-foot pole.

"Did he have kids?" I ask.

"Yeah. Mellie and Janice were teenagers. His

wife had her hands full. And I'm guessing they weren't full of the good doctor."

"We don't know that, Lovie. Besides, it doesn't matter. All we have to do is get the body back and go home."

It will be good to go back to my normal life. If you call *normal* worrying about sex with your ex and making fried peanut butter and banana sandwiches for a dog.

Although the restaurant isn't crowded and our booth is in the back, we wait until we're in the van before we lay out plan D—steal the body under cover of night.

"But I don't know how we're going to get in," I say.

"One of my many talents is picking locks."

"Holy cow. How do you know that?"

"The only good thing to come out of my six-week dalliance with Harry 'Slick Fingers' Johnson was learning to break and enter."

Sometimes Lovie scares me.

"I don't know how you figure that's helpful knowledge. It's not as if we're turning to life on the dark side."

"If your locked house caught fire and you couldn't find the dead bolt key, you'd find out. You ought to hear what I learned from Goober Jordan."

"I don't even want to think about it, Lovie. Let's go find a cooler."

We buy the biggest one Wal-Mart has, but even so, we're going have to bend Dr. Laton a bit.

Our next stop is the 7-Eleven, where we purchase enough ice to ice down three hundred pounds of shrimp.

"Even in the cooler, it's going to melt some in this heat," Lovie says.

"We'll get some more after we snatch the body."

I hate to picture the shape Daddy Laton's going to be in when we get him home. All I can say is Uncle Charlie has his work cut out for him.

Back in the van with the tools of our upcoming crime stashed in the cargo hold behind us, we break into a nervous sweat.

And it's only 4:00 P.M. By common consent we head to the ritziest mall we can find to shop. Buying shoes is the only way I know to keep my mind off my problems.

Well, that and sex. But currently, sex *is* my problem. Or one of them.

Four hours and three hundred dollars later, we head back to the motel with our packages—Dolce & Gabbana wedge heels for me and a Fredericks of Hollywood black bustier for Lovie.

Back in our room we change into all black suitable for burglary—slacks and long-sleeved T-shirts, never mind the heat.

There's no way we can return to our room lugging a corpse, even if he is wrapped in a tarp. Besides that, once we've got a purloined body in the back of Lovie's van, we don't want to hang around to see who gets pissed off.

We check out, and Lovie cranks up and rolls out of the parking lot. "Let's find a sixteen-ounce rib eye, Callie. We need red meat."

Wired on coffee and nerves, we head to Bubbles' house around midnight. Lovie leaves the van in a neighborhood park two blocks down the street, and then we skulk through backyards, darting from bush to tree.

Unfortunately, there's a full moon tonight, a little setback we hadn't counted on.

To top it off, we alarm a Pomeranian who sets up a commotion. Fortunately, the breed is too prissy to do more than bark.

I just hope nobody has a dog big enough to chew our legs off. Although I pride myself on being so good with animals I could be a dog whisperer, I'm not sure a Doberman would listen to reason if he caught us lurking in his territory.

All of a sudden, Lovie comes to a halt.

"Shit!" she says.

I bump into her. "What is it?" I whisper.

"I stepped in it."

"Well, wipe it off and come on."

I'm glad it's her shoes and not mine. Although my black Ponies are not pricey designer, they're cute and sassy and have become my favorite stealing-a-corpse shoes.

Finally we make it to our target. Every light in Bubbles' house is off. Lovie whips a hairpin out of her pocket and proceeds to break so we can enter. She's awesome. It's a pity I can't tell somebody about her cat burglar talents.

Two minutes later we sneak through the back door. In the path of moonlight coming through the window, we make our way to the freezer without bumping into anything, even the large box where Bubbles' cat is nursing newborn kittens.

I ease open the freezer's lid, and then Lovie and I grab the ends of the tarp and heft out the doctor's body. We're halfway to the door when my cell phone rings. We freeze, and the heavy body sags and almost hits the floor.

My phone keeps ringing and I'm almost wetting my pants. I'm fixing to be done in by technology.

Any minute now lights will pop on, Bubbles will attack us with a baseball bat, and cops will arrive to cart us off to jail. I can forget my unfortunate attraction to my almost-ex and my diminishing bank account. I'll have bigger problems—how to share a cell with hardened criminals.

I hold my breath, but nobody comes tearing into the utility room. Thank goodness for vodka-spiked lemonade.

Finally, my phone stops ringing. Leaping into action, Lovie and I sprint for the door and huff across Bubbles' backyard.

If I'd known a corpse could weigh this much I

might have rethought bringing Jack along as an accomplice. If I get through this caper alive, I'm getting into a hot bubble bath and staying a week.

Two years and a ruptured disc later (to say the least), we arrive at the deserted park. Both of us lean against the van, gasping for breath.

When she finds her wind, Lovie says, "Let's get this body in the cooler and get the hell out of Dodge."

More huffing and a protruding hemorrhoid later (I'm certain), we have the body in the back of the van.

"Quick, Lovie. Open the cooler."

She flips the lid and we start stuffing in the stiff when my cell phone rings again. I drop my end of the tarp and check to see who's calling while Lovie says a word that's not in my vocabulary.

It's Mama, so it must be an emergency. Even she doesn't make social phone calls at two o'clock in the morning.

"Mama? What are you doing up so late?"

"Some fool saw Elvis behind the Mooreville Truck Stop and called your house. I called Charlie and we found him courting a French poodle."

"Is he all right?"

"I guess so. Jack's got him."

"Jack! I thought he was in the Black Hills."

"Well, he's back, thank God. I couldn't deal with a lovesick dog and the Mims hellions, to boot. They're destroying your roses. Your garden looks like Hiroshima after the atomic bomb."

If I were the cussing kind, I'd say a word. Maybe three.

"Listen, Mama. We've found Dr. Laton's body and I can't talk right now. Tell Uncle Charlie, okay?"

I pick up my end of the tarp and we start stuffing again. "Good grief. He's not going to fit. Lovie, you may have to sit on the doctor and squash him in."

"Up yours."

"Let's reverse directions and put him in head-first."

The corpse bounces against the ice, the tarp parts . . . and we stare down at the cold, dead face of Bubbles Malone.

Elvis' Opinion # 4 on Freedom, Bachelor Pads, and Tender Loving Care

Ruby Nell and Charlie think they found me. I go ahead and let them believe their own fiction. It'll do them good.

Charlie's showing some stress over losing Dr. Laton's body, but it's Ruby Nell who has taken the brunt of it. She's so freaked out over keeping the Mims' teenage boys from destroying Callie's roses that she's taking her bedtime toddies at 3:00 P.M. and forgoing stylish outfits for blue jeans and baggy old T-shirts. She's even letting her roots show.

Of course, Callie will take care of that the minute she gets back. Which can't be too soon for me, in spite of the fact that I'm sitting here in the lap of luxury in my human daddy's apartment. I'm getting T-bone steak and scratched behind the ears every night. Plus, I'm getting to sit on his back porch and howl at the moon while Jack plays one of my biggest hits on his harmonica, "Heartbreak Hotel," which says it all.

Let me tell you, being a bachelor's not all it's hyped up to be. For one thing, Jack's dirty clothes are piled up high as my ears. Now, I like a good, ripe smell as well as the next hound, but his socks are over the top.

When he was married, he didn't have this problem. Callie used Bounce sheets in the dryer, but Jack's beginning to let the niceties slip.

For instance, he's got milk in his refrigerator as old as the Declaration of Independence and his cheese is growing mold.

Freedom's not all it's cracked up to be.

Personally I'd prefer to still be shacked up with Ann Margret getting a little tender loving care. And I'd bet the farm Jack feels the same way about Callie.

If he'd take some advice from me and whisk Callie off to some place exotic such as the Mooreville Truck Stop, he might put an end to this unfortunate marital rift. The two of them could be singing "Good Rockin' Tonight," that old hit from my Louisiana Hayride days, instead of sleeping in separate beds.

TLC, baby. That's what counts.

Chapter 7

Bengay, Diet Pepsi, and Murder

With the wrong corpse staring up at us, Lovie and I jump back so fast we crash into each other and land in a heap.

"Holy smoke, Callie. Are you sure that was the doctor's body you saw in the freezer?"

"It darned sure couldn't have been Bubbles. She was sitting on her sofa drinking spiked lemonade."

"If you thought going to jail for illegally transporting a body across state lines was tough, wait till we get the electric chair for murder."

Elvis will be homeless, not to mention the fact that Mama's out of Italian marble monuments and I'll end up six feet under a tacky tombstone.

"We have to put her back." I untangle myself and ease the tarp back over the wrongful dead. "Up and at 'em, Lovie."

She sits there like she's staking out a claim. "Callie, do you believe in bad karma?"

"We don't have time for religion. We've got to get Bubbles back in her freezer before she starts to thaw."

She's heavier going back than she was coming, or maybe it's the added weight of fear and crime. The Pomeranian knows us this time and runs up wagging her tail. But it's not dogs that subtract ten

95

years from my life; it's the car pulling into the driveway.

Caught in the headlights, Lovie and I drop to the ground. Car doors slam and snatches of drunken what-I-saw-at-the-party conversation drift toward the backyard.

Oh yeah, I believe in bad karma. I'm probably going to spend the rest of my life paying for this little misadventure.

In the time it takes this couple to get to the front door, I could have built Rome. Finally all is quiet and I nudge Lovie to see if she's still among the living.

"Let's go."

"I can't get up."

By the time I've tugged Lovie off the ground, the Pomeranian has taken matters into her own paws and has her teeth locked around Bubbles' wrist.

We try to shoo her off without setting up an alarm, but she won't let go.

"What's she doing?" Lovie asks.

"Not checking her pulse. That's for sure."

No manner of persuasion will make the little dog turn loose.

"What are we going to do?" Judging by the edge of hysteria in Lovie's voice, I'm soon going to have two prone bodies to worry about. She's not used to dealing directly with the dead, and she's about to crack.

I bend Bubble's arm so the little dog is now on top of the body, and we set off toward the freezer with the Pomeranian riding shotgun.

I can see the headlines: NATIONAL TREASURE OF FRANCE AND SIDEKICK ICE VICTIMS AND NAB SMALL DOGS.

The persistent Pomeranian doesn't get off till we're back inside the house. When she spies Bubbles' cat, the ensuing chase is enough to wake the dead. Everybody, that is, except our own unfortunate corpse.

It sounds like the battle of Armageddon. Lovie and I drop the body and give chase. Furniture waylays us right and left and the elusive animals outwit us at every turn.

"Lovie, let's herd the dog toward the door."

Using techniques we learned on the farm, I hold the door open while she finally flushes the Pomeranian outside.

"Poor old cat." I crawl under the kitchen table to retrieve the shivering Persian and take her back to her babies. "We ought to take the cat and kittens with us, Lovie."

"And get charged for catnapping?"

"They'll starve."

"We're not taking the cats, Callie. Let's get Bubbles back in the freezer before she turns to Jell-O."

As we stuff Bubbles back into the freezer I notice she's worse for wear. There are teeth marks on her wrist and she's all bent out of shape from trying to stuff her into the Igloo Ice Chest.

"I'm sorry, Bubbles."

"She can't hear you, Callie."

I like to think she can. If you can't love and be loved in this universe, then what's the point? I like to think the love surrounding the dearly departed lives on in some form. Maybe a star.

But now is not the time to get into it with Lovie.

"Cover her up and shut the lid while I feed the cats."

"The lid won't shut, Callie. Her arms are poking up. And there's *blood.*"

We never counted on rigor mortis, and certainly not murder. Apologizing once more, I squash Bubbles down in the middle, then rearrange the pork loins and chicken potpies so they fit in her lap. By myself. Delayed reaction has set in, and Lovie is in the corner threatening to lose her steak.

Suddenly I start to hyperventilate. Grabbing a pack of frozen peas, I dump the contents on top of the potpies and deep-breathe into the plastic bag.

Then it hits me. Lovie, the almost pro, wore gloves to break and enter, but my fingerprints are everywhere. We didn't count on stealing the wrong body.

I grab a dish towel from a stack on the nearby dryer and start wiping.

"Have you going crazy? Now is not the time to tidy up."

"I'm wiping my fingerprints."

"We'll never get them all off the tarp, Callie. Besides, I'm not touching it again."

"We'll just have to take it with us."

That means I have to do everything all over again. Solo. Which proves impossible with my eyes shut.

Calling on every known deity in the universe and a few I make up on the spot, I open my eyes, pry the tarp loose, and rearrange poor Bubbles with the spilled peas in her lap. Deprived of protection, she stares at me like a harpooned whale.

Somebody tugs my arm, and I jump to the moon. Thank goodness, it's only Lovie. "We've got to get out of here."

"Not till I feed the cats."

After I dump cat chow in the dish, we try to beat the dawn back to the van. By the time we get there, we're both in need of resuscitation.

Lovie slumps behind the wheel and I collapse in the passenger side.

"Lord," she says, and I say, "Amen."

Lovie's not above taking names in vain, but I can tell the difference. This is shorthand praying. We need all the help we can get. If we're going to get across the state line without being apprehended, it's going to take some divine intervention.

As we hotfoot it out of the neighborhood, every five minutes Lovie asks, "Do you see anybody following us?"

Each time I tell her no, even when I spot a police

car with red lights flashing. Fortunately the criminals on the lam are not us. He passes with sirens blaring and pulls over the car that whizzed by us a few blocks back.

"Why didn't you warn me, Callie?"

"What would you have done?"

"Put on lipstick."

This is the kind of laughter that kept me going when Jack swapped marriage for his Harley Screamin' Eagle.

"Break out the food," Lovie adds. "I'm starving."

Now I appreciate her foresight in packing. Add plenty of laughter and kindness plus a dab of financial security, and you could create world peace with Hershey's chocolate and Diet Pepsi. Lovie ought to be president.

It takes three chocolate bars to calm my nerves.

"Lovie, we have to find Dr. Laton and get him back."

"Are you out of your mind? As soon as Bubbles' body is discovered, who do you think the cops are going to come looking for?"

"All the more reason to stay and do some snooping. When we find Leonard Laton, we'll find the killer and exonerate ourselves."

"Who made you Sherlock Holmes?"

"The body's fresh—"

"Are you trying to make me throw up?"

"—which means the real killer could still be around here."

"Yeah, Callie, with an ax or a sawed-off shotgun or whatever he used to knock off Bubbles. I say we get out of Vegas before we land in more hot water than I can get us out of."

"I don't even want to know how you propose to do that."

"Why do you think I always carry a black thong in my purse?"

"I said I didn't want to know." And I darned sure hope Lovie's kidding. Though, after seeing her in action at Hot Tips, I'm scared to ask.

Up ahead there's a motel that looks like it caters to criminals and couples seeking love on the sly— no outside lights except the neon sign with the L and the A shorted out. The Blue Goon, it says, which seems prophetic to two neophyte criminals on the run.

"Quick, Lovie. Pull in here."

"Why?"

"This looks like a place you can pay cash with no questions asked."

"I have a feeling I'm going to regret this." She wheels into the parking lot and finds a space at the back. "So, what's your plan?"

"I don't have one." She says a word that makes me instantly apologize to God. "But I will tomorrow."

I tuck my hair under a baseball cap, wipe my mouth for any traces of lipstick, and untuck my shirt hoping to pass for a man. This is one of the few times I'm glad I was born under-endowed. If I've judged correctly, nobody will care that I'm sporting a lovely French tip manicure.

"Have you got your acting chops on, Lovie?"

"Why?"

"Because we're just another couple looking for an all-night romp."

"You are sick and must be destroyed."

Lovie links arms with me anyway.

Using Uncle Charlie's cash, I check us in as Dan and Gracie Jones. No questions asked. Thank goodness.

Our room is at the head of a set of stairs that creak under our combined weight. At this rate we don't have to worry about jail; we're going to end up toast on the cracked pavement. Shoving Lovie's head off my shoulder, I stave off death by leaping two steps ahead.

"Just for that, see if you score tonight."

"Shut up, Gracie, before I kill you."

Our room is lit with a bare bulb and looks like it was recently vacated by rats. I lock the door behind us and shove a chair against it.

"I don't think we have to worry about a plan, Callie."

"Why?"

"We're going to die in our sleep."

"Before I'm snuffed out, I want to be rubbed with Bengay." I ramble in Lovie's overnight bag for the tube. "I had no idea a corpse could be so heavy."

"If you mention that word again I'm going to throttle you. Go to sleep, Callie."

"Fat chance." I pull off my pants and crawl into the lumpy bed anyway.

Lovie's screech jolts me awake. I roll to the opposite side of the bed and grab the first weapon I find. Armed with a stiletto heel and expecting to stare into the face of death, I snap on the light. There's nobody in the room except me, still in the shirt I wore body snatching, and Lovie in an oversized T-shirt that says *Improve the Neighborhood, Invite Me to Dinner.*

"Where is he?"

"It's a bug."

"Holy cow, Lovie. You nearly gave me a heart attack."

"It's a *big* bug."

"I don't even want to talk about it."

In spite of the dubious cleanliness and the possibility of cockroaches lurking underneath, I'd like to crawl back under the sheets. We've had only four hours of sleep, and while I can still function like a halfway normal woman, my cousin has been known to spread terror when she's sleep-deprived.

"We'd better get moving, Lovie." Women on the lam can't afford to dally.

The only other time I've seen her move that fast

is Christmas morning. She's the only adult in the universe who still races to see what's in her stocking. Sometimes I think she never stopped believing in Santa—confirmation of my own belief that deep down Lovie is searching for magic.

After *Dan* and *Gracie* check out, we head to the nearest McDonald's drive-in window. Over Egg McMuffins I tell her my half-baked plan.

"I think we ought to find out what Bubbles' neighbors know."

"Bad idea."

"Why? If we can get a lead, we might find the doctor."

"If we go back there, somebody might recognize my van. And they can spot this red hair a mile away."

Lovie has a mane of natural curls that refuses to be tamed . . . and most certainly won't fit under a cap. She keeps it long because she says it's sexier.

I disagree. Take me, for instance. My sophisticated bob certainly rings Jack's chimes. But do you think Lovie will listen to a hair expert?

"I saw a costume shop across from Hot Tips. Wild Things and More."

"Callie, if you think I'm going in a gorilla suit, you've lost your mind."

"I was thinking of something more sophisticated. You in a black Cleopatra wig and me in a mustache. I don't think we should go back into Bubbles' neighborhood as two women."

"Then what? *Dan* and *Gracie* wouldn't have any business snooping around Cactus Street. I don't like this. Let's call Daddy and tell him the body has vanished again, then head home before we get hauled off to jail."

"Let me think."

As much as I would like to go home, get my dog, and curl up some place where I can forget about Bubbles and Dr. Laton taking turns in the freezer, I don't want to leave without trying to fix this mess.

I'm not one to walk away from problems. Except with my almost-ex, and technically Jack did the walking. Still, I wonder if I gave up too soon on my marriage.

I wanted to be like Uncle Charlie, who remains faithful to Aunt Minrose to this day, and Mama, who never even looked at another man after Daddy died. She could have had her choice of suitors but she turned them all away. *Michael's the only one for me,* she'd say, and I took for granted that all widows were like that.

Now, of course, I know better. Her love was so fierce that she'd rather have memories than another man. That's the way I loved Jack. Still do, I guess. And yet we've come to this terrible impasse that neither of us can bridge. Except with passion, and that just seems to have a life of its own.

"Callie?"

"Hand me another Egg McMuffin."

"I'm eating it."

"We got two apiece, Lovie." She pinches off a bite the size of a quarter and hands it to me. Pride is not my problem. I eat it. "You can be a reporter doing a story on the former showgirl and I'll be your male assistant. That way I won't have to talk."

"I wouldn't let us in the house, especially not without credentials."

"If you hadn't eaten my last Egg McMuffin, I could think."

Lovie pinches off another piece, and I nibble while I try to figure this out. If I'd known we would be forced to turn into Holmes and Watson, I'd have watched more detective shows on television instead of salivating over the Lone Ranger in a mask.

One thing is certain: we can't rent a car. That requires a driver's license. After trying to steal a corpse and messing up a crime scene, we don't want anybody in this town keeping records that can track us straight to Tupelo, Mississippi.

Chapter 8

Disguises, Discoveries, and Cat and Mouse Games

It's nearly lunchtime when we pull into the park near Bubbles' house. In the back of Lovie's van, I put on my mustache and clip my fingernails down to the nub while she dons a long black Cleopatra wig, Jackie O sunglasses, and a plain navy skirt with white blouse we bought at Wal-Mart.

On second thought, we decided it would be smartest to buy our disguises. When you're on the lam, you never know when you'll need to leave in a hurry.

Armed with notebook, pencils, and the latest copy of *Entertainment Today* magazine, we lock the van and head back to the scene of the crime. Fortunately, nobody is playing in the park. It's too hot.

Wearing my hair under the baseball cap and long sleeves to cover the feminine curves of my arms, I'm sweating like a sinner on the front seat of Boguefala Baptist Church.

The neighborhood looks relatively quiet—a few kids playing on the swing set two doors south of Bubbles' house, a tall skinny man with a cane walking a cocker spaniel, and a black Buick backing out of the driveway at the end of the street.

"Where to first, Callie?"

"Calvin. You might as well get used to it." I swing my head in both directions looking for the cops or a bright red Ford pickup. The street is empty. "Let's start next door to the crime."

"Shit. The Pomeranian."

The little dog sets up a ruckus the minute he sees us. Jumping around on his hind legs, he looks like he's trying to leap over the picket fence. The only good thing I can say is that he can't talk. The way he's acting, he'd definitely finger us.

"Sasha. Hush that racket."

A petite white-haired lady in pearls and Reeboks is standing on the front stoop shouting at the dog. I punch Lovie, and she trots over, leading with her winning smile and her big personality.

"Good *morning.* I'm Stephanie Wade from *Entertainment Today.*" She hands the woman the magazine opened to a feature on Brad Pitt with the byline, Stephanie Wade, in large letters. "We're here to do a story on your neighbor, the famous former showgirl, and we wonder if we could ask you a few questions."

"Who did you say you are?"

"Stephanie Wade. And this is my assistant, Calvin . . . Calvin Turnipseed."

"I mind my own business."

"It will only take a few minutes."

"I don't let strangers in, especially when my daughter's not home."

The elderly woman clumps inside and slams the door.

"Any more bright ideas, *Calvin?*"

"*Turnipseed?* What were you thinking?"

"That the Pomeranian was going to come over the fence and take a bite out of my ass. Let's go home."

"Not yet. Let's try across the street."

Lovie's not too happy about the prospect, but she goes along anyway. Thank goodness. My heart's not in this sleuthing business, either, but one of us has to show some grit or we'll never get Dr. Laton back.

We have better luck across the street. A woman the size of a Sherman tank with her hair dyed a dreadful orange I wouldn't even know how to duplicate shows us into a living room straight out of Tara. *Gone with the Wind* posters and memorabilia cover every wall and surface.

When she asks if we want something to drink, I feel like I ought to say, "Frankly, my dear, I don't give a damn." Instead I wait for Lovie to say, "That would be nice."

Our hostess leaves the room and Lovie elbows me. "Don't cross your legs like that."

"Why?"

"You look like a woman."

I slouch down in my chair and try to look like a rodeo cowboy. At least as macho as one named

Turnipseed can look. Which is the name Lovie gave this woman, too.

Returning with a tray holding tall glasses of something that's too dark to be water and too light to be tea, the woman who introduced herself as Marsha Simmons sets the tray on the coffee table and starts passing glasses.

"My own secret concoction. Exotic juices with a touch of spirits."

More than a touch, I'd say, which would account for Marsha's jovial mood.

"So, you know Bubbles well?" Lovie asks.

"I know every little move she makes."

That could be due to friendship, but I'm guessing it's due to the telescope at the window pointed across the street.

"Marsha, what's the first thing that comes to mind when you think of Bubbles?"

"Glamour. She sets the standard. Perfect makeup. Every little hair in place. Fabulous jewelry. She has a diamond necklace worth half a million. It once belonged to a queen. I forget who."

Holy cow. Could robbery be the motive for her murder?

"Great." Lovie turns to me. "Calvin, are you taking notes?" Laughing, she tells Marsha, "He's new. I don't know if he's going to work out."

Just wait and see if I let her take charge of the Egg McMuffins again.

"Tell me about her friends. Who does she see?"

"She talks about Divine and Bitsy Boobs a lot . . . they're showgirls, don't you know . . . but I never see them over there. She knows just about everybody. She even knew Frank Sinatra. And she practically worshipped Elvis Presley."

My dog would be in heaven, and frankly, I'm a bit proud myself. I'd like to quote Old Blue Eyes on Elvis—"I'm just a singer but Elvis was the embodiment of the whole American culture"—but my voice would never pass for male.

"People of her stature sometimes become reclusive. Has she seen anyone lately?" Lovie's a natural at this. But then, she's good at everything she sets her mind to.

"As a matter of fact, two women were over there yesterday."

I bear down so hard the tip of my pencil breaks. Lovie covers by proclaiming loudly that the drink is absolutely delicious.

"Did you know them, Marsha?"

"No, but they were probably stars of some kind." Marsha describes us with such accuracy she had to be looking through her telescope. "The tall one was too skinny for my taste, but that seems to be the rage."

I think I'm going to be sick, and not about the skinny remark. From the looks of things, Lovie's not doing too well, either.

I scrawl *License plate?* on the pad and show it to Lovie.

"If you saw their license plate maybe we could track them down. I'd like to get as much detail as possible for my feature."

"They were driving a pickup. No, I believe it was a van. From Minnesota."

"You're certain about the Minnesota plate?"

"Yes. Well, now. Wait a minute. I was busy looking at the sexy one's hair. I wish I could get mine that shade of red."

Lovie looks like she's getting ready to say *thank you,* and I elbow her. Any major blunders and Marsha will unmask us and call the cops. Fortunately a loud commotion outside saves us.

Marsha hurries to her telescope. Without a word, Lovie and I follow. Whatever is going on in this neighborhood, we need to know.

My nemesis, the big bad red Ford, is parked across the street. Its beefy owner is standing beside it talking to the woman in pearls and Reeboks while a crowd gathers and the Pomeranian barks his head off.

I think I'm going to throw up and Lovie looks like she's about to faint. I punch her ribs so hard she grunts. Still she doesn't say a word. I'm getting ready to punch her again when she recovers.

"I think we've finished here. Thank you for your time, Marsha."

"Wait. I wanted to tell you about the time Bubbles and I went backstage to see Elvis."

I write *number?* on the pad and hand it to Lovie.

"We're late for another appointment. Give us your number. We'll call you."

I wish we could ask *which way is the back door?* but that would draw attention to what is already a suspicious interview. Instead we walk out the front while sirens wail in the distance. I silently invoke every deity I know.

"Don't run, Lovie, and don't look back."

"Are the sirens getting closer?"

"Definitely." Blue lights flash as police cars round the corner. They whiz past while I'm trying to think of new ways to approach the throne of grace. Lovie jerks like a torpedo readying to be shot from the cannon. "Just keep walking . . . keep *walking*."

We reach the end of the street. Round the corner. Vanish from view of the LVPD. We breathe. Then break into a sprint.

Somebody must have moved the park to California. By the time we get there I can hardly hold myself upright, let alone imagine how we'll get out of this mess alive. Both of us lean against the van, heaving.

Finally Lovie recovers enough to unlock the doors. We leap inside and peel off.

"Slow down. We'll get a ticket."

If I repeated what Lovie says, I never would get the black marks erased from my record. She's sitting over there gripping the wheel with that *I told you so* look on her face.

We *didn't* find the body, or even discover a lead, but we did discover a possible motive for the murder—that diamond necklace that belonged to a queen.

"Which queen do you think Bubbles' necklace belonged to, Lovie?"

"If you say one more word related to murder I'm going to put your skinny butt out on the side of the road and let you hitchhike back to Mississippi."

"I wonder—"

"Callie, I'm warning you."

"—how long it will take my fingernails to grow back."

"I wonder where we can find a good rib-eye steak."

"Anywhere but Nevada."

Except for bathroom breaks and a hasty stop to change out of our disguises at an Exxon service station in Flagstaff, we don't stop until we get to Texas. Taking turns driving, we count the miles between us and Las Vegas.

When we finally sidle into the Boots A Walkin' Truck Stop to eat, I try to act as if I'm an ordinary tourist enthralled with cows and cacti.

The only problem is, I can't keep a nerve under my eye from jumping. And the way Lovie's scoping out the place, you can spot her a mile away. We might as well have "guilty" tattooed on our foreheads.

I poke her in the ribs. "Act natural."

"Like who? Your T-shirt's inside out."

"Why didn't you tell me sooner?"

"It was dark."

We slide into the back booth and try to discourage conversation, but just our luck, we get a waitress with more questions than the Gestapo. Lovie tells her we're FBI on a top-secret mission.

"One little leak could get us all killed." She gives the woman a dark look, and the poor hapless woman scurries off as if the knife is already in her back.

"I've got to call somebody about that cat," I say.

"The neighbors will find her."

"What if they don't?"

Lovie says a word I'm sure is not in the dictionary while I search for a pay phone. It's the long, dark hallway that leads to the restrooms. Phone books from Texas, New Mexico, Arizona, and Nevada hang from long chains attached to the wall. I call the LVPD to report a yowling cat at 106 Cactus Street.

"Who's calling, please?"

I tap my fingernails on the receiver and say, "My name . . . Smm . . . static . . . sorry," then hang up.

I'd feel like a better person except for one thing: I've failed Uncle Charlie.

As I slide back into my seat telling Lovie about the phone call, she shushes me and points to the wall-hung TV behind the cash register.

115

". . . discovered in her freezer. No details are being released. Police suspect foul play."

"We've got to get out of here," Lovie says.

"It'll look funny if we leave our food. Keep eating."

"What if we've been followed?"

"They'd have caught us before now."

We've lost our appetites so we end up discreetly (I hope) wrapping the steak in our napkins and stuffing it in Lovie's big purse so we won't call further attention to ourselves by asking for a doggie bag.

Back on the road, I drive while Lovie finishes her meal.

"I don't know how we're going to tell Uncle Charlie the body's still missing. I don't have a clue where to look now. And we certainly can't go back to Las Vegas."

"No. I'm a household word."

"As far as we know, only Marsha saw us, and she thinks we're from Minnesota."

"Yeah, but I mooned half the population of Las Vegas at Hot Tips."

"A truly unforgettable performance."

"Just shut up and keep driving."

I guess I would have run off the Mississippi River Bridge if my cell phone hadn't jolted me out of my stupor.

It's Uncle Charlie, welcoming us home.

"We're not home yet, Uncle Charlie. We're just crossing out of Arkansas into Memphis."

"Then how did the corpse get back in the casket?"

"Holy cow! The doctor's back?"

"He has a great deal of frostbite on his nose, and we'll have to retouch him and get him a new suit. Other than that, he survived his travels just fine."

"That's a testament to your embalming skills."

"Thank you, dear heart. But what happened out there?"

I give him a sanitized shorthand version, and I can tell you that unburdening your soul is everything it's cracked up to be, especially when the one taking charge is Uncle Charlie.

"All is well that ends well. You and Lovie be safe."

He's a big believer in the wisdom of great literature. Though I have this itchy feeling that Elvis' "Long, Lonely Road" best describes my future, I'm hoping Uncle Charlie and Shakespeare are right.

Elvis' Opinion # 5 on Marriage, Memoirs, and Sideburns

Callie's home. Don't ask how I know. I don't have these ears for nothing.

I may be barking up the wrong tree, but I think Jack should hustle over to her house with some chocolates and a nice box of Milk-Bones. A little show of faith that he's willing to do his part to work out this marital rift.

If it were left up to me, I'd have straightened out this mess a long time ago. I wasn't called the King for nothing. Folks closest to me know I reigned in the bedroom as well as on the stage. Look what I did for my pretty little wife up in Memphis. Put shag carpet everywhere and hung chandeliers. Genuine crystal. When you've got a woman worth keeping, you go all out for her. You make sacrifices.

Take Charlie, for instance. He walked on the wild side till he met Minrose singing down in New Orleans. The only thing that got him away from the seamy side of life was the love of a good woman.

Jack's the same way. If I told you what he does, I'd have to kill you. Suffice it to say when business brought him to northeast Mississippi and he laid eyes on my human mom, he naturally did what a man has to do. Wooed her, won her, and proceeded to settle down. Without a single thought about giving up his freedom or even giving up his job. He adjusted.

Of course, I wasn't there at the time, but I've heard these stories a million times. How he couldn't keep his eyes off her, how he thought she was the brightest thing in the park. When Jack first laid eyes on her, Callie was sitting in a lawn chair beside the lake at Ballard Park watching Tupelo's annual display of Fourth of July fireworks. The sky was lit up with a replica of the Stars and Stripes.

If that's not destiny, I don't know what is. Callie's the most patriotic human being I know—hauls her customers to the voting booths, decorates the little plastic tree in her shop with miniature flags every Fourth of July. And Jack has put his life on the line for his country.

He rescued her and she rescued him. Listen, these are two people who thought they were destined to be alone until that fateful night. He used to call her his angel of mercy and she used to call him her hero. Don't tell me they can't fix their marriage.

All they need is to listen to me. If Jack would grow some sideburns, he'd be a shoo-in with Callie. When I wore sideburns women threw their underwear at me.

What I ought to do is write my memoirs. Put my vast experience and good advice in a book. Callie might pay attention then. She's big on reading. Uses her library card all the time.

Of course, the library staff won't let me in. I have to sit in the Dodge Ram and amuse myself by guessing how long it will take the silly stray who hangs around Madison Street to figure out he's never going to catch the cocky jaybird in the magnolia tree by the Episcopal church.

I think I'll mosey around and see if Jack has a typewriter. Of course I could just march into his office and put the story of my life on his computer, but the romantic in me hankers for a good old-fashioned Remington. Pencils behind my ears. A good Cuban cigar. A splash of bourbon in my dog chow.

Chapter 9

Skullduggery, Moonlight, and Mosquitoes

My empty house hits me right in the heart.
Lovie offered to come in when she dropped me off, but I said *no,* I would be fine. Now I'm not so sure.

I walk to the closet to put away my shoes and get all choked up. There's still a big empty spot where Jack's clothes were. I stand there awhile remembering how he used to sit down in the rocking chair and pull me into his lap when I was blue. Then he'd rock me like a baby. Singing. Of all things. And he can barely carry a tune.

If I keep riding this train I'll turn into a soggy mess. I march right over and spread out the coat hangers so my colored blouses take up the room. A bare spot still eats at me, so I go into the bathroom to get my robe and hang it in the empty place.

Then I get in the Dodge Ram and drive down to see Mama. This is more than a visit to check on her and catch up on the news. This is a pilgrimage. When I feel beleaguered or even when I'm merely blue, I go down to the farm and let the land rescue me. No matter what happens, the land will not only endure, it will triumph.

That's the lesson I learn. As long as I can plant my feet on the patch of earth the Valentines have husbanded for generations, I will triumph.

Like the Native Americans, the Valentines know they can never own the land. They can merely take care of it so future generations can enjoy its beauty and largesse, can stand among its ancient oaks and listen to the lessons of the earth.

When the lake comes into view, I feel myself starting to relax, to let go, to slide back into my own skin.

Mama's sitting on the front porch with her feet propped up drinking sweet tea and watching a house wren who built a nest this spring in her hanging fern. When she sees me, she swings her legs to the floor.

"Don't get up, Mama. I'll get my own tea."

She has not only a big pitcher of tea in the refrigerator but also a lemon icebox pie. I cut myself a slice, pour a glass of tea, and join her on the front porch.

This feels like any other Sunday afternoon in August. If I could turn back time, I'd make the last few months disappear, starting with the day before Jack left me.

"What happened to your fingernails?"

"I chopped them off. Long nails get in the way of rolling hair."

I'm not about to go into details of our skullduggery in Las Vegas. Dr. Laton's back and we can return to normal.

Except for the tarp still rolled up in the back of

Lovie's van. And the possibility that she and I will be arrested for murder.

"Where's the Laton crew, Mama? They weren't at my house."

"They said something about taking the kids to the Buffalo Park. Good riddance, is what I say. Let Turf and Smurf terrorize the bison instead of me."

"I hope you didn't call them that to their faces."

"Do I look like I rolled off a watermelon truck?"

I'm not going to dignify that with an answer. Instead I send the universe a little hope that I can stay out of jail and live long enough to take my own children to such wonders as a sacred white buffalo in Tupelo, Mississippi.

"Callie, have you seen Jack?"

"No." I watch the wren take flight and land on the birdbath beside Mama's wisteria arbor. "After Daddy died, why didn't you remarry?"

"After Michael, they broke the mold."

"I know, but don't you get lonely? You're a beautiful woman, Mama. You could have found somebody nice."

"Who wants *nice?* I'll never settle for anything less than over-the-moon wonderful. And you shouldn't, either, baby girl." She leans over to pat my hand. "Besides, I have you and Lovie and Fayrene. And Charlie. He's taking me to dinner and the late show tonight."

"Have fun, Mama."

"Don't I always?"

After I leave Mama's I call Lovie on my cell phone.

"What did you do with the tarp?"

"Nothing yet. Got any bright ideas?"

"Burn it. We don't want a shred of evidence linking us to Bubbles Malone."

"And bring the Tupelo Fire Department to my backyard? No, thanks."

"How about the farm? Tonight around ten. Mama will be with Uncle Charlie, so she won't come running to investigate."

And the neighbors won't ask questions, either. In Mooreville, you mind your own business unless it involves juicy gossip.

When I get back to my house (which is still empty of Latons, thank goodness), I try to take a nap, but sleep is impossible. Instead I grab gardening gloves and my favorite spade, then head outside to tackle the weeds that are always trying to take over my garden.

The cocker spaniel bounces over to lick my feet and I turn into a big mass of crooning, babbling adoration.

"Hello, Dog. You cute thing. How's my little spaniel buddy?" I can't keep calling him Dog. He's going to get his feelings hurt. "What would you like your name to be?"

He sits on his fat little butt and puts his front paws in the air. Ever the entertainer.

"How about Hoyt?" Short for Hoyt Hawkins, who was one of Elvis' backup singers (The Jordanaires) in the 'fifties and 'sixties. Of course, my bassett will probably take umbrage. Elvis thinks he's the only famous entertainer on the block. Shoot, in the world.

Hoyt wags his tail and slathers me with doggie kisses, which I take as a sign he likes his name. Now that I've named him, he has probably graduated from *stray* to one of the household, which is not a bad thing. Maybe he can help take up the empty spaces.

A few minutes before ten Lovie picks me up and we head down to the farm. I have to get the tarp out of the van by myself because she refuses to touch it again. She picks up sticks for kindling while I drag it from the van. Thank goodness, it's too dark to see the blood.

I squash the tarp in a wad, Lovie throws some sticks on top, and I strike a match. The kindling ignites and we stand back to watch the evidence burn.

The only problem is, the plastic is thick and heavy. Instead of turning into flyaway ashes we can scatter around the pasture, it's hardening into tight, blackened nuggets.

"Throw on another stick, Callie. That wadded-up spot is fizzling out."

I stumble around in the dark looking for fallen

limbs. If I find a snake I hope he's the polite kind who believes in live and let live.

After I toss in enough sticks to stoke the fire to inferno proportions, Lovie and I try to cool ourselves with cardboard fans-on-a-stick she's been hauling around in her van since the last Valentine family reunion at Wildwood Chapel. They feature a picture of the Garden of Gethsemene, where all sorts of skullduggery took place. I just hope they're not prophetic. I don't fancy being at the wrong end of mob justice.

"I liked Bubbles," Lovie says. "We had a lot in common." I don't even want to think about what. "Who do you think killed her?"

"It could have been anybody." I tell Lovie about meeting the creepy Buck Witherspoon in the rain on Mama's farm and Uncle Charlie's reaction. "Do you know anything about him?"

"Never heard of him. I could ask Daddy."

"No. Let it go. Uncle Charlie's been through enough."

I throw another stick on the fire, not because it needs more kindling but because I need to stay busy so I don't have time to think about my recent crime spree.

"Besides," I add, "I don't believe in coincidence. Whoever killed Bubbles found Daddy Laton in the freezer when he stowed the body, then decided to put him back in the casket. I can't see Buck caring what happened to Dr.

Laton's corpse. The logical murder suspect is one of the family."

"Janice seems too flighty to carry out cold-blooded murder. And as mad as she was over the will, I can't see her dragging her daddy all the way across the desert to lovingly restore him to the casket. Besides, wouldn't Aunt Ruby Nell have noticed if Janice went missing from your house?"

"What about Kevin? He didn't get completely cut out of the Laton fortune, but Bubbles took the bulk of it."

"Maybe. But judging by my undercover work, I'd say he's more interested in loving than killing."

If I get started on Lovie's undercover work, I won't stop. You can't reform somebody who's not interested in changing. I learned that from trying to steer Mama away from mahjong and into macramé. But I still keep trying with Lovie. And hoping.

"I don't think you can rule Kevin out," I tell her. "And then there's Mellie. What do you think about her?"

"She's too prissy and timid. I'm betting on Bevvie. She's still at large with her arsenal of weapons."

"Yeah, but how would she know where to put her daddy's body?"

"Maybe one of her sisters has been in touch with her without telling us."

"I still think Kevin is the logical choice. He

didn't react at the reading of the will. Ordinary people aren't that poker-faced. What do you know about him, anyway? Besides the obvious."

"He's some kind of executive at the hospital."

"Doing what?"

"How do I know? It's not like he's part of Tupelo's old guard. He's only been here three years. Remember?"

Lovie met him at a hospital benefit she was catering. He was the handsome new guy in town, which made him the man most likely to find Lovie's favor. She'd already cycled through most of the local bachelors, some of them more than once.

"See, that's what I'm talking about. You only know what Kevin told you. There's no telling what he does at the hospital. And where did he move from, anyhow?"

"I guess I could try talking to him. It might be an interesting change of pace."

"I don't think you ought to see him again, Lovie. He could be a killer."

"He's a killer, all right."

"I'm serious. You could be putting your life in danger."

"This is creepy, Callie."

"You're right. Besides, we don't have to worry about it. Bubbles is back in the freezer, Dr. Laton is in Eternal Rest, and Elvis is home."

"What about these big wads of wrinkled-up plastic?"

"Oh, shoot."

The only thing to do is borrow a bucket from Mama's back breezeway, dump water from the lake on the fire, then throw the incriminating charred remains into the lake and hope they sink to the bottom.

And don't kill the catfish.

By the time we've finished, Lovie and I look like Tar Baby and have mosquito bites the size of Texas.

"I'm not cut out for a life of crime," she says.

It's not a life of crime I have on my mind right now. It's how I'm going to get the soot off my Cole Haan shoes and how I'm going to get Elvis back without ending up in Jack's bed.

I know, I know. With rampaging problems like global war, hunger, and murder, I'm a shallow person for thinking of shoes and sex. But you have to start somewhere. If you can't keep everything in your own backyard in order, how can you expect to fix the disorder of the world?

While we're watching the last of the tar balls sink to the bottom, Lovie says, "Poor old Bubbles. It doesn't seem right taking her funeral pall and leaving her in the freezer with peas in her lap."

"It's a tarp, Lovie. Besides, what else could we do?"

"Maybe we ought to sing her a song."

"Now?"

"Well, yeah. It can't hurt. Maybe she'll forgive

us. She might even put in a good word with Saint Peter."

"We didn't kill her, Lovie."

"I know that. Still, it was our fault the Pomeranian chewed on her."

I start singing in a shaky soprano, and Lovie joins in with a lusty alto. I'll have to say we sound pretty good. Of course, we've had years of practice. Mama and Aunt Minrose started us singing duets at Wildwood Chapel when we were kids.

My voice gets stronger as I go along, and I feel like a better person. If there ever was a song that can redeem you—no matter what—it's "Amazing Grace."

Chapter 10

Fleas, Fitness, and Mayhem

After we leave the lake, Lovie drops me off at my house to get my truck and I head straight to Jack's, never mind the condition I'm in. The only way I can get settled back into my routine is to retrieve my dog.

Elvis sets up a ruckus the minute I pull into the driveway. Jack's lights are still on and I can see my dog jumping up and down at the second-story window.

I park the Dodge Ram under the only tree on this desolate-looking, cracked-pavement lot—a scraggly little pine turning brown at the top. Pine beetles, would be my guess. If they keep on chewing, before you know it Jack won't have a single tree and I can add *deprived my ex of simple pleasures* to the list of guilt I carry around like Janice Laton Mims' Prada purse.

Jack loves nature. He could sit in my rose garden for hours and not say a word, just sit in our white wicker rocking chair smiling. Last summer when it got so hot and dry it felt like Mississippi had turned into the Sahara, he was the one who watered the roses.

"Let them go, Jack. Maybe next summer will be better and I'll plant more."

He kept on watering. Maybe he knew something I didn't. Maybe he intuitively knew that, for us, there would be no next summer.

Jack left me right before last year's Christmas holidays. Just thinking of that awful Christmas makes me swap my guilt for righteous indignation. Living in a tacky yellow brick apartment building on the wrong side of Tupelo serves him right.

Magnolia Manor, it's called, which brings to mind mint juleps served on a gracious patio with a view of tennis courts and English gardens. Obviously the person who named it was delusional. The only view is the pitiful pine and the rundown putt-putt golf course next door.

I priss right up and punch the buzzer like I mean business.

133

"Jack, it's me."

He wastes no time buzzing me up.

"My God, Callie. You look like you're back from the dead."

He doesn't know how close he is to being right.

"Don't mind me. I just came for my dog."

Elvis skids into the hall and starts licking my feet and legs. I squat down and scratch his ears, then hide my face in the soft fur on top of his head. Mostly because I love my dog, but partly because I don't want Jack to see me crying.

Listen, I'm only human. Sometimes all this gets too much. Why can't life be simple? Why can't it just meander along without husbands and dogs and corpses disappearing on you?

When I've pulled myself together, I stand up and say, "Go get your toys, Elvis. Let's go home."

Jack grabs my arm and hauls me inside. "Sit. I'll make you some hot chocolate."

"It's ninety degrees outside."

Naturally he pays me no mind, just stalks into the kitchen and starts banging around in cabinets. It's like having God take charge. All I can do is sit there and contemplate my sins. Which are myriad. If they keep adding up, I'll have to hire a secretary to keep track.

All this stress makes my head hurt, and I'm not even the kind of woman who has headaches. Next thing you know I'll be developing Fayrene's fireballs in the useless and losing interest in shoes.

The seductive smell of chocolate wafts from the kitchen, and I lean back and close my eyes. This feels so good I might not move till after Dr. Laton's funeral or for the next two years, whichever comes first.

Holy cow! It's the crack of daylight and I'm in Jack's bed, naked as a boiled egg. Even worse, I can't remember a thing after I smelled that chocolate.

Jack's not on the other side of the bed, which means he could be lurking anywhere. I ease out and tiptoe around searching for my clothes. If I hurry I can be dressed and maybe sneak out of the apartment with my dog.

Dognapping again. I wonder if Jack can use that against me in court.

I can't even find my T-shirt and shorts, much less my underwear. When the lights blare on, I'm on all fours feeling around under the bed, naked. I pop up and crack my head on the bedrail. If I were Lovie I'd say a word that starts with D. Maybe even F.

"You're up."

"Of course. I have business to attend to." I rise and give him the once-over as if I'm Venus surveying her conquest from a personal seashell.

I'm not about to cave in and ask him the whereabouts of my clothes, and I'm certainly not going to ask him what happened in this bed.

It would be just my luck to have caught some weird form of temporary amnesia from the chemicals exuded by that burning tarp. Maybe even temporary insanity.

"Since you're up, I'll make breakfast."

"Jack Jones, if you think I'm going to follow you to the kitchen like a bassett hound puppy, you've got another think coming." I jerk the sheet off and wrap myself up, sarong-style. "Elvis and I are leaving."

"Don't you even want to talk about last night?"

Shoot. If I'm going to keep falling off the wagon with my almost-ex, the least I want is to remember the fun.

"I hate to disappoint you, Jack, but it was forgettable."

He laughs so hard I want to slap him. Instead I tag after him trailing the bedsheet. His apartment is a mess. Socks wadded up and tossed everywhere, T-shirts draped over the backs of chairs, Chinese takeout boxes piled on the coffee table.

Plus, a wrinkled sheet and a pillow with a slept-on dent on the sofa.

The sight makes me want to cry. Even worse, I want to straighten up, spritz with Fabreze, add paintings to the walls, bake a pan of gingerbread so the apartment smells of cinnamon and home.

Lovie calls me the earth mother type, and I guess she's right. Otherwise I'd be scheming how to get Jack's silver Jag in the divorce settlement instead of trying to figure out how to clean his apartment without sending off the wrong signals.

He takes my clothes out of the dryer, never mind that his own dirty jeans are piled knee-high.

"If you're leaving, put these on. I need my sheet." With that, he undoes the knot and strips me bare. "Such a waste."

I could say a thing or two about who left and why, but I don't. All I want is my dog and my underwear.

I turn my back to put on my clothes, but not before I see Jack's grin. "Where's Elvis?"

"Asleep in my bathroom."

Jack dangles the key over my shoulder, then keeps standing behind me so close I can smell Irish Spring. I used to stand in the shower and rub the soap on his back.

Okay. Now I'm weak at the knees. If I look at him, I'm likely to end up spread across his table like raspberry jam on bread.

"He's not safe with you as long as that French poodle is in a courting mood. Besides, he misses riding on my Harley, and his back-alley girlfriend gave him a case of fleas."

"I'll take him to the vet."

"No. *I'll* take him to the vet."

Jack turns me around by the shoulders and looks at me like I'm a hot jelly roll and he can't wait to dig in. If I don't get out of here fast I'll end up parked in Lovie's green kitchen eating chocolate and confessing wicked misdeeds. Again.

Jerking myself free, I stalk out. When I get in the Dodge Ram and notice that Jack washed the soot and grim off me and even put pink calamine lotion on my mosquito bites, I almost go back inside and do his laundry.

Of course, that's not all I'd do. I peel out and head home.

Janice Laton Mims is sitting on my front porch swing with my autographed copy of *Fried Green Tomatoes at the Whistle Stop Café,* wearing my blue piqué robe and drinking from my favorite coffee mug with writing on the side that says the power of the spirit is even more amazing than the wonders of nature (my personal philosophy).

If I'd known Mama was going to let them take over my house, I'd have left Uncle Charlie in charge.

Janice gets up and puts her hands on her hips like I'm the maid.

"I was wondering where you were. We're out of ground coffee. I had to drink instant."

I pretend she never said such a tacky thing to me. "Good morning. How are you?"

"Disinherited. Ready to kill my sisters. Does that sum it up?"

"Oh, is Bevvie back?"

"I don't know the whereabouts of either one of

them, and I don't care. All I want is out of this god-forsaken place."

She flounces back into my house as if I've personally deprived her of California. Besides, I take umbrage at her slurs on Mooreville. True, nobody would call it cosmopolitan, but it has its virtues. I can't think what they are right now, but after I've worked off some steam at the gym I'm likely to sit down and make a list and present it to Miss High and Mighty Janice.

I grab my gym bag and punch Lovie's number on the way out the door.

"Lovie, I'm on the way to the fitness center. Do you want to work out with me?"

"I'd as soon grow nose hair. Besides, I'm making cheese straws and cream puffs for the Ladies' Social at Calvary Baptist."

The fitness center sits on a hill on the south side of Tupelo's sprawling medical complex—a deliberate ploy to make you think twice about getting off the stationary bicycle before you get your body revved up enough to fight off clogged arteries and other diabolical malfunctions.

The thing that sends me scurrying back to the dressing room in a near-trauma is not the looming prospect of terminal illness; it's the sight of Mellie Laton puffing away in the weight room and Kevin Laton doing laps in the pool in the atrium. I'm so tired of Latons and their problems

I'd give up cute shoes to be rid of them. Well, almost.

I grab my bag from the locker and don't even take time to change out of gym clothes. Leaping into my Dodge Ram, I peel out of the parking lot and head for the nearest exit home.

It's my house. If Janice is still on my swing, I'll make her sit in the rocking chair.

Cliff Gookin Boulevard is clear of early-morning traffic. You can make record time getting around town if you don't get stopped by one of the many trains that block Tupelo's major arteries at obscene times, i.e., when you're already late for a dental appointment on the other side of the track or you're suffering chest pains and need to get to the hospital before you die.

I'm driving along minding my own business and thinking about work where the most upsetting thing I'll encounter is a hair dryer on the blink, when out of the blue somebody rams my back bumper. And me, on the bridge! If I weren't in this giant piece of kick-ass metal, I'd be flying over the railing to Glory Land.

When I get the wheel under control, I glance in the mirror and see a Ford F-150 four-by-four. Blood-red. A driver the size of an Iowa State line-backer, his baseball hat pulled low.

"Holy cow!"

It has to be the same man who was trailing us in Las Vegas. I don't know of another truck around here that's pure testosterone. Except mine, of course. I bear down on the gas pedal and shoot forward like a raging bull.

My escape is short-lived. The Ford plows into my rear end again. Glancing in the rearview mirror, I see the driver has his head hung out the window, gesturing toward the side of the road.

"Pull over!"

I shoot him the bird and whip out my cell phone. If I live through the next two minutes, I'm calling 911.

Elvis' Opinion # 6 on Back Roads, Bologna Sandwiches, and Firearms

You wouldn't expect a man as worldly wise as Jack Jones to get all shook-up over a woman, but then you don't know my human daddy. He may look and act like a tough guy, but let Callie show up and he's just a big hunk a' burnin' love.

If he had listened to me this morning and picked her a nice bouquet of goldenrod instead of locking me up in the bathroom so I couldn't go back home with Callie, he'd have had her washing his dirty socks by now.

Listen, love me tender has its place, but I have priorities just like the next dog. When you have to open windows to keep from being gassed by the smell, it's time to take action.

The only action Jack takes is to hit the open road. Now, I'm not saying I don't like to be all suited up in my doggie helmet with the lightning bolt across the front, strapped to my little seat and watching the trees whiz by. I'd be lying. In spite of the string of starry-eyed canines I've wooed with "I'm Yours" when all I meant was "It's a Matter of Time," I pride myself on truth.

I'm about to tell Jack a thing or two about women when he wheels into this ugly trailer park on the south side of Fulton and parks under the shade of a magnolia tree.

"Sit tight, Elvis."

Bless'a my soul. The next thing you know Buck Witherspoon strolls out and gets in his green extended-cab Chevrolet. Jack tails him all the way across the Alabama state line. Things are getting interesting till Buck pulls into a fast food restaurant. We pull right in behind him and Jack orders two bologna sandwiches without consulting me.

I could be snooty and hold out for a hamburger, but I decide to cut him a little slack. Any man who mishandles his marriage the way Jack has deserves a little TLC.

We take our sandwiches back to the Screamin' Eagle and Jack whips out his cell phone.

"I've got him, Charlie . . . No, he's inside a Jack's hamburger place east of Hamilton, Alabama . . . Okay, I've got it covered from this end."

Looks like I'm the point man in a stakeout operation. I might have to back Jack up with a firearm. Contrary to what most folks would imagine, I'm good with guns. Back when I had sideburns and women throwing scarves at me, I had my own shooting range.

Bring on trouble, baby. I'm wild in the country and rarin' to rumble.

Chapter 11

Killers, Cream Puffs, and Casinos

The dangerous stranger whips out from behind and zooms along beside me, never mind that he's in the oncoming traffic lane.

"Want to talk," he yells.

"Calling cops," I yell back, then proceed to dial 911. By the time I get *help* out of my mouth, the Ford F-150 has swerved left onto Veterans and disappeared. I blurt out my story till I'm stopped cold with the question, "Did you get his tag number, ma'am?"

"No, I was too busy fighting for bladder control."

There's a snicker on the other end, and I watch my chances of collaring the killer plummet to zero. There's a number for you.

I'd pull over to the side of the road and hang my head out the window, but the killer could be lurking around waiting for his chance to do no telling what all.

I turn around in McDougal Center's parking lot and head straight to Lovie's house.

When she doesn't answer the doorbell on the fourth ring, I let myself in with the spare key she hides under a faux frog on the front porch.

"Lovie?" No answer. I nearly have a coronary. "Lovie, are you home?"

"In here."

She's teetering on a four-foot ladder scrubbing globs of goo off the kitchen ceiling.

"Holy cow. What happened?"

She turns toward me and the ladder tilts dangerously toward the left. I grab hold and anchor her.

"I saw somebody at the kitchen window."

"Who?"

"How do I know? An intruder. I went after him with a meat cleaver. While I was crashing through the bushes, my cream puffs exploded."

"How did that happen?"

"I accidentally set the platter on a hot eye."

The ladders lists again, groaning this time, and I have to fight to keep Lovie from crashing into the sink.

"Get down from there. I'll clean while you hold the ladder."

"What are you doing here this time of day? I thought you had beauty shop appointments this afternoon."

"Not till two." While I scrub I tell her about my brush with death, ending with the conclusion that I think the would-be killer is the man we saw in Las Vegas.

We piece together a timeline and figure the mysterious stranger would have had time to destroy Lovie's peace of mind plus her culinary creation, then whip over to Cliff Gookin and scare the pants off me.

"Somebody's trying to kill us, Lovie."

"But why? We haven't done anything."

"Except lie, impersonate the Folies, break and enter, and tote a murder victim across public and private property."

"You think it's all tied in with Bubbles?"

"I don't believe in coincidence. It's not only tied in with Bubbles, it's somehow tied in with the corpse that won't stay put."

"Is Dr. Laton still in his casket?"

"If he's not, I don't even want to know."

"What are we going to do now?" Lovie plops onto a chair, too upset to mention chocolate.

"Search the yard for clues."

"Not without a weapon."

Lovie grabs a knife big enough to carve Texas, then hands me a toilet plunger. Armed to the teeth and filled with false bravado, we head outside to search the bushes.

"What are we looking for, Callie?"

"I don't know. Maybe he snagged his pants on the lantana bush. Or dropped a matchbook cover with a phone number written on the inside."

"While he was at it, maybe he left his business card."

"Sarcasm doesn't become you, Lovie."

"Neither does murder."

Sobered by that thought, we redouble our search

efforts, but turn up nothing except an earring Lovie lost last May.

I ask her how it got in the bushes, but she just shrugs her shoulders and asks, "What are we going to do now?"

"If we're going to get ourselves killed, we'd better tell Mama and Uncle Charlie."

After Lovie and I drop off cheese straws and the surviving cream puffs at Calvary Baptist, we convene at Eternal Rest with Mama and Uncle Charlie. He insists on the viewing room so he can keep an eye on the corpse with wanderlust. Fortified on strong coffee and leftover cream puffs, Lovie and I take turns telling our morning's horrors.

"I think it's all connected, somehow," I say.

"Lord, I nearly lost you." Mama falls on me like I'm the fifty-cent table at a yard sale. "I don't know how I'd survive it."

"Now, now, Ruby Nell." Uncle Charlie pats her on the shoulder. "'Virtue is bold and goodness never fearful.'"

He has fallen back on Shakespeare again. *Measure for Measure.* The funny thing is, it miraculously restores Mama's equilibrium.

"I haven't been good in twenty years, Charlie, and I'm damned sure not virtuous."

She stomps into the kitchen and brings back a bottle of Baileys Irish Cream, which she liberally splashes into her coffee.

"We should all disappear," she says.

"We have a body to bury, dear heart."

"Not till Bevvie's found. Besides, when's the last time you took a vacation, Charlie?"

"It's hard to leave here. People are always dying and they count on me."

"It's high time to hire that assistant you're always talking about. Leave that old two-timing turd in his hands and let's all take a restorative trip to the casinos."

There go my afternoon's profits.

"You know, Ruby Nell, one of these days I might just take you up on that."

Uncle Charlie lifts the coffin's lid to make sure Dr. Laton is still put, then pours everybody a second round of coffee. We all get up and add Baileys.

Having spiked coffee and crumpets around a coffin is not your everyday sort of social, but the Valentine family takes a more broad-minded view of death. Lovie even goes into Uncle Charlie's office and puts on a Muddy Waters CD.

"Might as well enjoy some good music while we plot," she says.

Gutbucket blues and a haunting harmonica blaring over the speakers can make you forget everything. Except murder.

"There's only one solution I can see," Uncle Charlie says. "We've got to catch the killer. And fast."

"Lovie and I couldn't even bring home the body, Uncle Charlie. How do you expect us to find a killer?"

"All of us, dear heart. Let's figure out the motive and go from there."

"Money," Lovie says. "Remember the diamond necklace Marsha mentioned."

"Marsha who?" Mama asks; then Lovie has to reveal our escapades in Las Vegas. I notice she leaves out the part that featured her in feathers.

"If you'd carried me to Las Vegas, I could have busted this thing wide open. I speak their language."

I know what Mama would have *busted*, and that's my bank account. She's sitting there puffed up, daring me to explain how I could be such a thoughtless daughter. I kick Lovie's shin, and she kicks me back.

But she gets the message. "We didn't want to put you in danger, Aunt Ruby Nell. Come to think of it, the motive could be revenge or love."

"How do you figure that?" I ask.

"TV reruns of *Matlock*. I've learned a lot about detective work from them."

"Still, that's a far cry from apprehending somebody with a gun."

"Was Bubbles shot?" Uncle Charlie checks the corpse again, as if Dr. Laton might have pulled a Houdini within the last five minutes.

"I don't know. There was lots of blood. Coming

from the back of the head, I think, but I didn't look. Did you, Lovie?"

"Do I look like somebody with the red badge of courage tattooed on my butt?"

"Ruby Nell and I will go to the courthouse to check out the written copy of Leonard's will. While we try to find out who would get the money if Bubbles dies, you and Lovie scout around to see what you can hear. And be careful."

"Lovie, why don't you move in with Callie till all this is over? I'll ask Jack to keep an eye on you."

I kick Lovie again, and she says, "I'll be fine, Aunt Ruby Nell. Don't worry."

"If we're not going to do the sensible thing and run to Tunica, then letting Jack move back in is the next best thing."

"I'd rather take my chances with a cold-blooded killer, thank you very much."

Mama's never going to admit defeat. And I'm not sure she'll ever forgive me for depriving her of her son-in-law. She loves Jack as if he's her own flesh and blood. And I can see why. He's wonderful to Mama, one of the many reasons I fell in love with him in the first place.

Still, just because he's good to Mama doesn't mean he's father material. Even if he does have the preliminaries down pat.

I head off toward Mooreville, checking the rearview mirror every three seconds for any signs of the Ford. I can't wait to get to the relative sanity of Hair.Net.

But first I stop by the house to change shoes. I'm happy to report Janice is not in my porch swing. I sit in it and smell the gardenias awhile. Just because.

Feeling better already, I go inside and listen for the sound of loudmouth Laton/Mims. Blessed silence greets me. This is good and bad. Good because it means my houseguests are not here and bad because I don't hear the patter of plump Elvis paws.

I search through my closet till I find just the right perky shoes, a pair of Manolo Blahnik leopard-print sling-backs with fake-jewel buckles. Not your typical afternoon-in-the-beauty-shop shoes, but I pride myself that I've never aspired to be ordinary.

Add a yellow sundress and a pair of dangling leopard earrings with faux emerald eyes, and I can almost forget history nearly repeated itself this morning on the Cliff Gookin Bridge.

After I put fresh water in the pets' watering dishes and spread treats all around, I head toward my beauty shop.

Who should be waiting for me but Jack astraddle his Harley?

I'm glad I wore the sundress. Yellow is one of my best colors.

See? This is what he does to me—makes me forget I hate him.

"I see you've brought Elvis home."

"I have."

I'm afraid to believe my ears. Instead of saying something and giving Jack a reason to change his mind, I act as if I expected Elvis this afternoon, anyhow.

"Since it's so hot outside, you might as well come in and have a cool Diet Pepsi."

"I had something more scintillating in mind."

"Not unless you want to be caught with your pants down. Fayrene will be here in ten minutes for her color touchup."

He passes me and nabs a Coca-Cola from my refrigerator.

"I meant a cold drink, but I like the way you think, Callie."

"Did you know that when you lie to me, your eye twitches?"

Jack puts on his sunglasses while Elvis trots past both of us and sinks into his plush doggie bed with a big sigh.

"He acts tired."

"We've had a busy morning."

"So have I."

"I heard. Elvis and I are moving back in."

This is just like Jack to tell instead of asking. Which is one of the things I used to love about him—his take-charge attitude. That just goes to show that if you judge through the eyes of love, you're bound to miss a few crucial flaws.

But on the flip side, if you err on the side of caution and analyze every little thing, you'd miss an awful lot of pleasure. Though Jack's moved out and I'm moving on, I'm still not sorry for all those years I spent with him.

"I'm taking Elvis, but if you think I'm going to let you move back in and impersonate a husband, you're sadly mistaken." He looks like a mountain standing there, inviting and endurable, something you'd want to crawl next to and curl up in a little ball. "I mean that, Jack."

"I know you do, Cal."

He runs his finger around my lips, then leans down and kisses me. And shoot, if I don't end up kissing him back.

"Later, baby." He pats me on the butt, then climbs on his Harley and roars off.

I march right into my office and call the locksmith. I'll be darned if I'll let a brush with death and a conspiracy between Mama and Jack upset my plans to liberate myself from him while I still have viable eggs.

Fayrene walks in right in the middle of me telling the locksmith this is an emergency. Translation: Jack still has a house key.

"Did somebody break in?" Before I have time to answer she adds, "There's been a lot of that going around here lately. Somebody tried to break into Bitsy Cleaver's house last week, and her right in the middle of singing Acapulco."

A capella. Saints preserve us.

But Fayrene's gossip does give me a chance to dig for clues. If houses are being robbed, is it possible the theft of Dr. Laton's body was merely a random act?

But still, how did it end up in Bubbles' freezer?

"Does the sheriff have any suspects?"

"Bitsy described a tall man."

"Heavyset? Wearing a baseball cap?"

"Well, Lord, yes. I think so."

"Do they know who he is?"

"Come to think of it, Bitsy called him *weasely.* But I don't think that's his name. He was wearing a hat. And driving a green pickup."

Shoot. That lets out the red Ford guy.

I go into the washroom to mix Fayrene's color and nearly jump out of my skin. There's a man silhouetted through the glass of my back door. Grabbing the nearest weapon—my haircutting scissors—I head in that direction.

"Who's there?"

My yell brings Fayrene and Elvis running.

"Good Lord, Callie. What are you doing in here talking to the mop?"

She opens the back door and rehangs the mop that has blown loose from its moorings. Once I settle in to work on her hair, I'm back to myself in no time. Especially with Elvis lying at my feet, scratching his ears.

"Does that dog have fleas? There's a new vegetarian in town. Jarvetis thinks he's the next best thing to God. He wouldn't take his bird dogs anywhere else. He's kin, too. My cousin June's nephew's wife's first cousin once removed."

If you're from the Deep South, you can eventually rake up a family connection with anybody.

Making a mental note to ask Jack if he's already taken Elvis to a veterinarian, I set about making Fayrene's hair color the envy of everybody in Mooreville who has the bad judgment to go to another beauty parlor.

Chapter 12

Sweet Tea, Motives, and Ménage à Trois

Home again after my first day back at Hair.Net, I was hoping to find my house empty of guests so I could settle down to some quality time with Elvis, then turn on my computer and Google the Laton offspring. Instead, it's overrun by Latons. Janice has commandeered my porch swing again, her boys are ripping through my roses, Bradford is in one of my porch rockers, and Kevin has taken up residence in the other.

Taking umbrage at this invasion, Elvis lifts his leg on Kevin's tires, then sulks off to chase the cats away from his favorite spot in the shade of a large blackjack oak in the backyard. I make sure to shut the gate behind him.

"Boys, please make sure this gate stays shut. I don't want Elvis to come up missing again."

Janice's teenagers look at me as if I'm speaking a foreign language. I am six feet tall in these heels and can look taller if I try. I march straight over to my rosebushes, tower over them, and give them a look that hints of guillotines in their near future.

"He's a very valuable show dog, and if he gets out I'll deal with you personally. And stay out of my roses."

The next thing I do is go onto my front porch and reclaim my swing. When I plop down right in the middle, Janice gets up as if I'm typhoid fever and she's never been vaccinated. Marching across my porch like the Queen of Sheba, she makes Bradford get up and let her have the rocking chair. He stations himself behind her. By now he's probably used to this subservient position.

They've already helped themselves to my sweet tea, so I don't offer a drink. As irritated as I am at the loss of privacy, I can't let this opportunity pass to dig for information that might lead to a cold-blooded killer.

"I'm sorry you're having to wait so long for the funeral."

"I could shoot Bevvie," Janice says. "She ought to be the one having to wait around in this wretched heat." Bradford tries to moderate her with a hand on her shoulder, but Janice spews on. "And I could kill Bubbles Malone."

I wonder if that means she *did* kill her, somehow escaping Mama's not-so-vigilant eye, or if she doesn't even know Bubbles is dead.

"She seemed like a nice woman." I think it's bad karma to speak ill of the dead, and besides, I want to prod Janice again to see just how far she'll go.

"That witch took every penny Daddy had. She ought to be shot."

"I thought she was charming in a quirky sort of way," Kevin says.

He doesn't sound like a man who recently stashed a victim in a Frigidaire chest freezer, but maybe he's just cleverly trying to cover it up.

"Did you know her?" I ask.

"I heard Mother mention her name a time or two."

"Kevin. Shut up!"

"Janice, I think I heard Uncle Charlie say you used to live in Las Vegas."

"Oh God, spare me." Janice shoots out of her chair and storms into my house, slamming my door so hard I'm sure she warped the hinges. It'll take me a week to get my house back in order after they leave.

Bradford calls after her, "What do you want me to tell Mellie if she calls?"

"Tell her to go to hell."

"I'm sorry," he says, then trails along behind his wife.

"Did I step on somebody's toes?"

"It wasn't you, Callie. Let my two older sisters out of their cages, and there's bound to be a cat-fight."

"But why is Janice so mad at Mellie?"

"She's furious because Mellie has been holed up and hasn't returned any of her calls. You don't ignore Janice and get by with it."

Kevin unfolds himself, and I can see why Lovie's so attracted. There's a seductiveness about him that goes beyond good looks. He exudes danger and power. Jack's major two qualities that both madden and mesmerize me.

"Thanks for the tea."

If he leaves I may never get another chance to question him. And I surely don't want to leave that to Lovie. She'd be alone and in the dark, while I'm here in broad daylight with a house full of witnesses and a fierce watchdog at my command. Elvis may not look the part, but don't let his stature fool you. Once he stood off a pit bull who tried to make me his next snack while I was outside tending roses.

I casually follow Kevin to his car, hoping to come up with a brilliant plan to extract further information. If I'd known sleuthing would be this hard, I'd have given in more when Lovie wanted to watch old detective reruns instead of always insisting on westerns and musicals.

"Come back anytime," I say.

"If you're suggesting something kinky, Callie,

I'm game. We'll grab Lovie and head out of town."

I picture an abandoned barn and Kevin armed with a black whip. And a hacksaw. Holy cow. I'm fixing to get us both killed.

"Jack's moving back in."

"Maybe he'd like to watch."

"He'd slit your throat."

Luckily Kevin leaves before the locksmith arrives. Unluckily, Mama arrives hard on the heels of the van with *Ernie's Locks* printed on the side.

She bails out of her car bustling with news and bad advice. I can always tell whether Mama has come to ask for money or to advise me of the error of my ways. If she wants money, she dresses down—pale pink lipstick and fingernail polish she thinks make her look wan, plus one of her more subdued caftans in nice, matronly colors. Eggshell blue or baby pink. Funereal beige, if she's really trying to get my sympathy.

"We need to talk," she says, then proceeds to stand around with her hands on her hips watching Ernie change the front door lock.

Finally she says, "If you're planning to keep Jack out, you're wasting your time."

"I never waste my time, lady."

"I don't recall saying a word to you. I was talking to my daughter." She grabs my arm and tugs me toward her car. "Get in."

"I can't leave while the locksmith is here."

"We're not leaving. I just want some privacy." I

climb in on the passenger side and Mama cranks up the car, then turns the air conditioner and the radio full blast. "I have news."

"Shoes?"

"News!"

The upstairs bedroom curtain parts and I see Janice peering out. Even worse, Fayrene pulls up behind us in her glow-in-the-dark hearse.

Tapping on Mama's window, she shouts, "Ruby Nell, are you all right in there?"

"We're fine," Mama screams. "Just listening to some good jazz."

"Well, good Lord, why don't you get out of the car? You're going to have a heat frustration attack."

You can hear them all over the neighborhood. Probably even in the next county. I reach over and turn off the radio, then roll the windows down.

"Mama was just showing me the short in her radio. Thanks for stopping by."

Fayrene doesn't leave till she shares her new recipe for pecan pie. Then I roll up the windows and ask Mama to please get to the point before somebody calls out the National Guard.

"Charlie and I found a copy of Leonard Laton's written will, big as you please."

"And?"

"If Bubbles dies, all the money goes to charity."

I'm not sure about that. When Mama's excited, she sometimes gets facts mixed up with her own fiction.

"Where's Uncle Charlie?"

"At the funeral home. Gertrude Harris died."

"Poor old soul. What did Uncle Charlie say about the will?"

"There goes motive down the drain. His exact words." Then without skipping a beat, she says, "If you're not careful, your marriage is going to follow suit."

"Personally, Mama, I'd be happy to flush it."

"Well, your loss is going to be Leonora Moffett's gain." Mooreville's answer to Lady Chatterly. "She's after him, and once she gets her claws into a man, she doesn't let go."

"I don't want to hear it."

"Fine, then." Mama turns the radio back on and proceeds to sit there tapping her fingers against the steering wheel.

"I didn't mean to hurt your feelings, Mama. I just don't see the point, that's all. Come in and have some tea."

"I'll pass. I have important things to do."

I hope they don't involve roulette wheels.

As soon as Mama and the locksmith leave, I put Elvis on a leash under the guise of walking my dog so I can have a cell phone conversation without being overheard by the nosy Janice.

Elvis has to make his mark on every mailbox on the street. It takes me fifteen minutes to get around the bend and out of sight.

"Lovie, what are you doing?"

"Painting my toenails."

"What color?"

"Purple."

It's not her best shade, but Lovie gravitates toward the color preferred by royalty.

"Can you get over here and take Elvis to the vet? His French poodle gave him more than love."

Elvis pays me back by hiking his leg on Leonora Moffett's prize day lilies. I yell, "Stop" and pull him off before the damage is done.

On second thought, maybe he was eavesdropping, too, and is just taking his revenge on Jack's latest conquest.

"What are you going to be doing, Callie?"

"Making poor old Gertrude Harris look like Greta Garbo." Her last request to me before her family carried her to Memphis for shock treatments. "Besides, you owe me a favor, remember?"

"Okay, I'll pick him up in fifteen minutes. By the way, I Googled Kevin."

"And?"

"When he was eighteen he was arrested for drunk driving and disturbing the peace. His parents were in Europe with Bevvie, who was sixteen at the time. Guess who made his bail?"

"Who?"

"Bubbles Malone."

"Which means he lied when he said he didn't know her."

I give Lovie the lowdown on my front porch

163

sleuthing and Mama's discovery at the courthouse; then we make plans for tonight.

After I finish at the funeral home, we're going undercover again to find out what else Kevin is hiding with lies.

You'd never believe this, but some of my most relaxing times are spent with the deceased at Uncle Charlie's funeral home. Maybe it's because my uncle has turned this old house into a place that provides just what the name says—Eternal Rest.

There's something warm and inviting about the room where I work. Uncle Charlie painted it soft pink and added wall sconces with shell-shaped plastic shades, a French-style makeup table, an end table with a lamp to match the sconces, and a comfortable sofa covered in mushroom-colored velvet. As a finishing touch, I brought throw cushions in gold, hot pink, and red.

Sometimes I get the feeling the deceased are looking down at this homey setting and nodding their heads with approval. I hope they're also pleased that we treat them with respect.

Propping a picture of Gertrude's idol on the makeup table, I say, "Don't you worry, Gertrude. Uncle Charlie and I are going to take good care of you."

I'm putting the finishing coat of pancake on her face when the door creaks open. I jerk around and my makeup base rolls onto the floor.

"Sorry, dear heart. Did I scare you?"

"Thank goodness, it's you. I'm just a little jumpy, that's all."

"I have to oil those hinges."

Uncle Charlie sits on the sofa and opens a slim book titled *Native American Wisdom*.

"Don't mind me." He puts on his reading glasses and starts to read.

Though he usually comes down to keep me company when I'm working, there's a different purpose about him now, a firm set of his jaw that gives off dangerous signals. I'd hate to be the one to cross him.

I don't know if it's my intense love for him or my newly frayed nerves, but I'm unusually observant today. Suddenly I'm struck by how handsome he is. And how alone.

As far as I know, he's never looked at another woman since Aunt Minrose died. I wonder if that's partially my fault. And Mama's. We were both so needy after Daddy died, he couldn't have had much time for himself.

"You should find somebody, Uncle Charlie."

"I have my family, dear heart."

"I mean somebody to marry. Or at least a companion."

He puts the slim book down, then stands up. "I have to go upstairs and check on Leonard."

The door hinges squeak again, and I get the feeling I've stepped into forbidden territory with my uncle Charlie. Who am I to give advice on love?

Instead of telling him to find a companion, I should have asked him what made his love for Aunt Minrose so strong. What made their marriage endure beyond the grave? Maybe I could have learned a thing or two that would help me figure out how Jack and I ended up with a train wreck instead of a future.

Suddenly I glimpse movement outside the window. Pulling the lacy curtain back, I strain my eyes into the growing dusk, but all I see are the two giant magnolia trees on the other side of the parking lot.

Going back to the table, I set to work creating the deep red bow-shaped lips and almond-shaped eyes of the 1920s movie diva.

Something heavy drops on the floor above me and I nearly jump through the ceiling. The heavy clanking comes again and I race up the stairs screeching for Uncle Charlie.

Greta Garbo will have to wait.

Elvis' Opinion # 7 on
Doctors, Pissants, and Dignity

They can't fool me. I know when I'm going to get a vanilla-ice-cream cone and when I'm being hauled off to the vet.

The only reason I didn't protest when Lovie picked me up is that she understands bribery.

I trotted off to her van like there was no tomorrow. I can smell a greasy sack a mile, but I'm smart enough to know that if I touched it before we were out of Callie's sight, there'd be a big price to pay.

If she knew I was fixing to scarf down a dozen doughnuts, she'd never let Lovie take me anywhere again. Plus, she'd cut my dog chow down to something that wouldn't even satisfy a cat.

When we peeled out of the driveway, I hung my head out the window and howled Callie a few bars of "Always on My Mind." Listen, I'm not the kind of dog to let my head be turned by Krispy Cremes and joyriding with my ears blowing in the breeze.

Then I buried my head in the bag Lovie handed me and went to work.

Now Lovie is taking a curve doing seventy-five and I'm jerked out of sugar-overload heaven. A lesser dog would have slid off the seat. I just hang my head out the window and watch the countryside whiz by.

I wish Lovie would slow down. Details are

blurred. Plus, my digestion is not what it used to be. Back when I was a young buck, I could eat fish bait so well seasoned by the sun the Moffett's dumb shih tzu down the street wouldn't touch it. The only consequence I suffered was having to chew foul-tasting green breath-freshening bones before Callie would let me back in the house.

My whole system's in rebellion against my big appetite. By the time I realize we're going the wrong way, we're somewhere on Highway 371 heading north toward Mantachie.

"I'm taking you to see that new vet. Luke Champion."

That's all right with me, Mama. The last time I went to see Dr. Sandusky, Callie left me there for the day and they put me in a roomful of pissants. I mean, really. What self-respecting dog is going to embarrass his human mother by sitting in a cage and howling? These mutts were carrying on so, I was ashamed to be canine.

Take a little pride. That's what I say. Show some dignity.

We pull up to this nice-looking country house, yellow clap-board with a big front porch, and at first I think I'm off the hook: Lovie's going to visit somebody I don't know and spare me the indignity of having my fleas documented.

Up until now, my record has been clean as a whistle. But if I had it to do over, I'd do it all again. That little French hottie was worth it.

Then I see the sign and I know I'm going to have to suck it up and get this over with. The wooden shingle hangs in front of a freshly painted concrete building off to the side of the house, and features pictures of animals. The dogs and horses add a touch of class, but personally, I could do without the cats. Why ruin the neighborhood?

We're ambling up to the door, taking our time, stopping so I can take care of a little business on the petunias. Then the doctor walks out and Lovie metamorphoses into a bona fide seduction machine.

I don't trust a man that good looking. Especially a blond. My human daddy can hold his own with the best of them, but he's a hundred percent man's man. A scar or two, hair a little long and always stirred up by the wind, nose a bit crooked where he broke it nearly getting himself killed down in Mexico.

We go inside and I'm getting ready to lift my leg on the doc's statue of a dog peeing on a KEEP OFF THE GRASS sign, when he scoops me onto the table and says, "This basset's a fine specimen."

Now, I like compliments as well as the next dog. The doc's reputation inches up a notch.

Next thing you know, he zooms right to the top by telling Lovie, "This is my favorite breed."

Here's a man who knows his canines. I'd be willing to bet if I stick around long enough, he'll figure out I'm the King.

Chapter 13

Locks, Spies, and Victoria's Secret

I top the stairs and head down the hall toward Uncle Charlie's office so fast I lose one of my Steve Madden moccasins. But I'm not about to stop to retrieve it. There are worse fates than running around on one shoe. For one thing, running around without a head.

Any minute I expect to have mine chopped off.

Where is Uncle Charlie? I'm screaming so loud it's a wonder Dr. Laton doesn't rise and try to give me Prozac.

I skitter down the hall, peering into viewing rooms. They are all empty except the one that contains the late doctor.

Thanks goodness his coffin's still there. And on the floor is a heavy length of chain. I'm fixing to be shackled somewhere and tortured for burnt ends and bad haircuts. Accidental, of course. Nobody's perfect.

All of a sudden I realize I'm frozen in the hallway outside the good doctor's room, fresh bait for anybody with a pair of sharp scissors and a yen for revenge.

Screaming for help, I race toward the front double doors. But what if somebody's out there in the dark, waiting?

"Oh, Budda, Great Spirit, Holy Mother, and holy cow, if I get out of this mess alive I'll give up sex." My poor unused eggs rise in protest, and I amend that. "But only with Jack."

I hear footsteps behind me and nearly faint. Instead, I set out running again. And calling to every deity in the known universe.

"Callie! Wait."

Collapsing in a little heap, I begin to hyperventilate.

Uncle Charlie cups my shoulders. "Breathe, dear heart. Just breathe."

When I'm coherent I ask, "Where were you?"

"I heard a noise and went outside to investigate."

"I heard it, too." I stand up, shaky but in one piece. "Did you find anybody?"

"No. Not a sign."

"Wait till you see what's on the floor in Dr. Laton's viewing room."

"Wait till you see what's in his casket."

Stuck to Uncle Charlie's side like Velcro, I skirt around the chain and peer into every corner for somebody with an ax. Probably a man in a baseball cap.

Or it could be a woman with a Prada purse?

Uncle Charlie is oblivious of the chain, and for the first time in my life I see him as growing old. Losing his eyesight. His hearing.

Please, I think. Just that. *Please.*

Flinging open Daddy Laton's casket, Uncle Charlie says, "Look at that."

I don't know what I expected to see. Maybe the return of Frigidaire frostbite. Certainly not the red pasties. And most certainly not the matching G-string.

"Hoy cow! When did that happen?"

"While I was downstairs with you and poor old Gertrude. Whoever did this is slick. And fast."

"Also dangerous. Did you notice that chain?"

"That's mine, dear heart. When I saw these in Leonard's casket, I went down to the basement and found something to stop this nonsense."

He whips the pasties and G-string onto the floor and starts wrapping the casket with chains. Only then do I see the enormous lock on the end.

"Nobody gets in this casket again. Or out. Unless he's Houdini."

"So it was you who dropped the chain?" He nods, too busy setting his escape-proof trap to do anything else. "Are these the same pasties that were in the casket the first time?"

"I haven't had time to look." He grabs a handful of chain and tugs. The casket rocks but the shackles remain in place. "That ought to take care of our problems with vanishing corpses and unwanted going-away gifts."

Then he puts his arm around me, leads me upstairs, and seats me in a rocking chair before he checks on the first set of red pasties. They are still in his bureau drawer.

"I can understand Bubbles' killer putting Dr. Laton

back. But if it's one of the Latons, why on earth would they keep putting red pasties in the casket?"

"We're probably dealing with at least two people who have different agendas. I'm going to talk to Jack."

Before I can remind him that Valentine family business is no longer Jack's business, Uncle Charlie has gone to the kitchen. And since when did they become such cronies, anyway? Uncle Charlie always liked him, but I didn't think they were confidants.

In a few minutes he comes back with two fat mugs of hot green tea chai.

"Drink this. Gertrude's viewing is not until Wednesday. You can come back tomorrow and finish her. Let's put all of this out of our minds for now."

I'm still shaking and hot chai spills on my hands. Uncle Charlie wipes it off with his handkerchief, then notices my bare foot and goes back downstairs to retrieve my missing shoe.

When he returns he puts on his glasses, takes out a thick blue volume, and begins to read aloud:

"When in disgrace with Fortune and men's eyes,
I all alone beweep my outcast state,
And trouble deaf heaven with my bootless cries,
And look upon myself and curse my fate . . ."

I know Uncle Charlie is trying to soothe me with poetry—and succeeding. But I also know how

Shakespeare's Sonnet 29 ends, and I wonder if he's remembering my advice and showing me that age has a wisdom only the young can dream of.

> *"For thy sweet love rememb'red such wealth*
> *brings,*
> *That then I scorn to change my state with kings."*

Remembering the Uncle Charlie of my childhood, I see him bending over Aunt Minrose while she's at her baby grand piano, offering her a freshly cut rose, the dew still on its petals. And I see their faces, lit with a tenderness that stopped me in my tracks and held me behind the living room door, heart racing.

I wonder if I'll ever know a passion such as that. Or have already known it, and let it slip through my fingers.

After I leave the funeral home, I drive to Lovie's. She meets me at the door with Elvis, who looks suspiciously content. Usually after a visit to the vet, he gnaws a few chair legs to get even.

"How did it go, Lovie?"

"He's a dreamboat. An absolute hunk."

"Elvis?"

"No, the new vet. When he put his hands on Elvis, it was all I could do to keep from crawling onto the examining table, myself."

"What happened to Dr. Sandusky?"

"Elvis hates him."

"How do you know?"

"By looking at your furniture. Are you going to stand in the door quizzing me all night, or are we going spying?"

While I update her on the latest doings at Eternal Rest, we don Uncle Charlie's hats and wigs from Aunt Minrose's stage days. With jet-black curls springing out from my felt fedora, I look like a werewolf doing Phillip Marlowe.

When we planned this stakeout, we decided to go incognito, and I guess the disguises are working. Elvis sees us, and his hackles rise about three inches.

I soothe his ruffled feelings, then ensconce him on the sofa with a Milk-Bone and his favorite TV show, *American Idol*. He likes to howl along.

Armed with binoculars (my idea) and a meat cleaver (Lovie's weapon of choice), I tell Elvis to be good and guard the house. Then we climb into my Dodge Ram and drive off.

"What's wrong with Elvis?"

"Nothing. Why?"

"I've never seen him ignore a doggie treat."

"I already gave him one."

"Not too much, I hope. Dr. Sandusky says if he keeps gaining weight, I'll have to put him on a fitness diet."

"Champ didn't mention a diet."

"Champ?"

"The new vet. Luke Champion. That's his nickname."

I don't even want to know. Besides, we've arrived at our destination, the subdivision on the south side of Tupelo where all the streets are named for presidents.

Kevin's one-story brick house is on Eisenhower, which I think is the main reason he was doomed with Lovie from the start. She's a yellow-dog Democrat, and here he is living on the street named after a Republican icon.

Made wiser by our Pomeranian encounter, we decide to avoid backyards. I park two blocks from Kevin's and we mosey down the sidewalk.

"This wig is hot as the devil." Lovie scratches her head so hard she reminds me of Elvis before the flea treatment.

"The wigs were your idea."

"Do you have a better one?"

"No."

"Then hush up and pretend you don't see that patrol car."

It pulls up beside us, and a flashlight shines in our faces.

"Do you two ladies need any help?"

"No." Lovie hides her meat cleaver in the folds of her skirt and flashes her famous smile. "We're just out for a stroll."

This is the first time I've seen her charm fail. Probably because her wig is turned sideways.

"Is that your Dodge parked down the street?"

"We've been visiting my aunt on McKinley," I tell him. "We were heading home when my friend got a cramp in her leg. We're trying to walk it off."

Lovie hops up and down on one foot—a sight to behold. With a warning to be careful, the streets are no place for ladies this late at night, the officer tips his hat and leaves us to our misdeeds.

"Hustle, Callie, before we land in jail."

Lovie powers off and I have to trot to keep up with her. Putting on the brakes when we near Kevin's yard, we tiptoe toward cover, scrunching down so we're out of the pool of light coming from his window.

The two of us (combined width, the approximate size of a small Toyota) attempt to hide behind a hydrangea bush (two feet max, even with the blossoms). Branches creak and pop in our wake, and to my guilty ears they sound like the crack of doom.

We freeze, expecting Kevin to come out the door with a gun. But all is quiet so we hunker down and get to the business of eavesdropping.

"Somebody's with him," Lovie whispers. "A woman."

"Can you hear what they're saying?"

"No, but I can guess . . . and it's not for the faint-hearted. Can you see who it is?"

"Wait a minute." I shift a limb out of my way and clear a bird's-eye view of Kevin's living room. "It's Mellie. Crying."

"Why?"

"How would I know? Shh. Wait a minute." I press closer to the window and catch a snatch of conversation. "They're talking about Bubbles . . . and Bevvie. Holy cow!"

"What? What?"

"They used the word *murder*."

"Let's get out of here. I don't want to be their next victim."

We hotfoot it out of there, leaving behind two murder suspects and a mutilated hydrangea bush. Back in the van, Lovie spends ten minutes recovering her breath while I spend it recovering from a near heart attack. To say the least.

"Bevvie did it," Lovie says.

"We don't know that for sure. I still think Janice is the only one with enough venom, and Kevin is a known liar."

Still, Bevvie is in parts unknown. Suddenly I remember an article in *Field and Stream* featuring a picture of the youngest Laton offspring with a pile of poor dead ducks at her feet. Tomorrow I'm going to Google the rest of the Laton heirs to see what else I can discover, especially about the family's big game hunter, Bevvie.

If I live that long.

After I drop Lovie off and tell her to deadbolt every door, I head toward Mooreville with Elvis. Even though he snoozes the whole way home, I'm glad I won't have to walk into my dark house alone. Especially with a killer on the loose and my suspicions it could be the one sleeping in my guest bedroom.

Listen, I know it might have been smarter to stay somewhere else, with Lovie or Mama or even Uncle Charlie, who tried to persuade me. But if I'm now the target, why put the rest of my family in jeopardy? And if both Lovie and I are next on the list, why give the murderer an opportunity to kill two birds with one stone?

Anyhow, I'm stubborn. I'm not fixing to let anybody run me out of my own house. Besides, I have Elvis. He's not what you'd call an attack dog, but at least he'd bark and give me enough time to arm myself.

I let myself in with my new key, then bend down and caution Elvis to be quiet going up the stairs. The last thing I need is Janice waiting in the dark to pounce and quiz me. Or worse.

Most people who've had the traumatic day I did would skip the bedtime ritual, but I'm not the kind of woman to let beauty and good grooming slip. Besides, my hair is stuck to my scalp from sweating under Aunt Minrose's wig, and I look like Rudolph Valentino wearing too much Alberto V05.

After my shower and shampoo, I spend a full ten minutes with Oil of Olay. At my age any less is just asking for premature crow's-feet.

"Come here, boy." Elvis trots over for his good night petting, and then we both fall into bed.

I am not alone.

Somebody has pinned my arms to the bed and clamped a hand over my mouth. I flail around, trying to get loose.

Where's my dog and why didn't he wake me? I'm going to be front-page news. MOOREVILLE'S MOST FAMOUS HAIRSTYLIST ATTACKED IN HER BED.

"Don't scream."

The whisper is close to my ear. I shiver, then get hot all over. In places you don't want to know about.

"Are you going to keep quiet?"

"Hmmm."

Jack releases me, then brushes a kiss on my shoulder. "Good girl."

"How did you get in?"

"Picked the locks."

"If you'll care to remember, this is my house."

"I know."

"I ought to call the law."

"But you won't."

His hand is on my leg, sliding under my gown. I know I ought to make him leave. And I could. He's not the kind to force his attentions.

I have only one thing to say on the subject: I'm glad I'm wearing Victoria's Secret.

Chapter 14

Guns, Strangers, and Man-eating Trollops

I never thought I'd be packing a pistol. But here I am on the farm before any decent rooster would think of stirring, pouring bullets into the air around a bale of hay with Jack's .45. Not only that, I'm sporting a leg holster he had strapped on me before I was awake good from a lovely dream that featured me floating through the air behind a line of baby carriages.

On the positive side, all I can say is that Jack had me out of the house before any of the Latons woke up.

I don't see the point of all this, and I've told him so. He said it was to keep me safe, but I have a news flash. After this Laton business is cleared up, the only dangerous thing I plan to do is be the first one crashing through the doors for McRae's Labor Day shoe sale so I can get to the Cole Haans before they're picked over.

I've never had to use a weapon for that. Though at times it's tempting.

I squint and take aim again, this time blasting a hole in the oak tree. Jack just stands there, obviously awed by my skill.

Finally he says, "That tree was six hundred yards away from your target."

"Yeah, but I hit it, didn't I?"

"The point is to hit your target. Don't think about it, Callie. Just point and shoot."

"Like that will help me if I'm looking into the eyes of a cold-blooded killer."

At the rate I'm going I'd have my leg shot off before I could get the gun out of its holster.

"Okay, let's try something else." Jack wraps his arms around me from behind and stands so close you couldn't get a straw between us.

If I'd known this target practice was going to turn X-rated, I've have put on a chastity belt. Or my cute new thong.

Putting his hand over mine, he swings my arm and squeezes the trigger. Bull's-eye.

"How did you do that?"

"You did it, Callie. Now. Again."

He repeats this motion till I think my arm will fall off. Suddenly I've blasted the target before I'm even aware that he's no longer pulling the trigger.

He takes the gun, reloads it, then hikes up my skirt and rams it into the holster.

"Stay out of trouble, Callie. I have business to take care of."

I wonder if his business involves Leonora Moffett (Mama's bad advice fomenting), but I'd cut off my tongue with my favorite haircutting scissors before I'd ask. I have better things to do than stand around being jealous of every woman who looks at Jack sideways. Besides, it would take me about fifteen years because that includes every woman in Lee County except Fayrene and Mama.

After Jack drops me off and I pick up Elvis, I head to Hair.Net and power up my computer to search cyberspace for clues. This takes a while because I'm still on dial-up. Though some would say differently, Mooreville is not the center of the universe and not exactly top of the list for fast Internet access service. In the middle of my typing *Bevvie Laton* into the Google search engine, my computer heaves a big sigh and goes to that great computer roundup in cyberspace. Permanently, it looks like.

I predict another big hole in my expenses, and I don't even need a gazing ball.

There are some places you can't get by with a gun, even if Jack Jones did tuck it up your skirt. Lee County Library is one of those. You can't even take your dog in there.

I had to leave Elvis with Mama.

After I finished transforming poor old Gertrude to Greta Garbo at the funeral home, I headed to the library for more sleuthing. I could have used Uncle Charlie's computer or Lovie's or even Mama's, but after being with Jack all morning—and night—I felt the need for some real solitude so I could repent without family commentary.

Finding a computer in the corner as far away from everybody as I can get, I start scanning newspapers for articles on Bevvie Laton's nefarious activities. Listen, don't talk to me about sport. I'm a dog mother.

An article from Florida shows Bevvie all decked out in hunter green with guns that would give you nightmares, her foot propped on an alligator the size of my recliner. I'd say she's not a woman to mess with. I'd say she'd be more than a match for Bubbles Malone.

Then I see an article from Montana that gives me the shivers. After printing it out, I Google Janice. She's not the news maker Bevvie turned out to be, but she is high enough in society to warrant a few inches of print.

Her wedding got a big spread but yields no clues. The only article of any significance is about a charity benefit Christmas ball Janice hosted. There's nothing interesting here except a picture of a crowd scene with Janice in the forefront sporting a bad haircut and a salmon-colored gown with red lipstick that clashes.

I'm about to move on when I notice a face in the background that looks vaguely familiar. When I press ENLARGE, the woman comes into view—big hair, lots of cleavage, too much eye makeup. It's Bubbles Malone.

I print the picture, then move on to Mellie. Apparently she never married. If she had, wouldn't there have been a big society wedding like her sister's?

I find an article from Las Vegas about her senior prom—a posh event sponsored by Dr. Laton, featuring the Latin rhythm band of Juan Cheveros, who billed himself as successor to Xavier Cugat, the Rumba King. In the picture, Dr. Laton is flanked by his wife, his daughter Mellie—who was surprisingly pretty as a teenager—and Mellie's escort, a large, handsome guy with a shy smile. He couldn't have been the band director because he's obviously not Latino; plus, he's not named. That means he also didn't have enough blue blood to be considered newsworthy.

He looks vaguely familiar, though I have no idea why. This picture is nearly thirty years old. I was a mere child then. Still, I'm getting a funny vibe, as if I'm missing something important.

I print it out, and race to my Dodge Ram. Forget Googling Dr. Laton. I barely have time to share this news with Lovie before I head to Mooreville for my next appointment. I wouldn't even take the time to call her, but if I'm the next victim, I want somebody to know what I know.

"Lovie, what are you doing?"

"The question is *who*."

"Good grief, not Kevin Laton."

"I decided to pump him for further information."

"You're going to get yourself killed."

"What a way to die!" I hear dishes clanking; then Lovie says, "Anyway, he just left and I'm making brandied peaches. What's up?"

"I've Googled the rest of the Latons. Janice knew Bubbles."

"How do you know?"

"I have a newspaper picture of Bubbles attending one of her charity benefits."

"Wouldn't it be open to anybody who bought a ticket? That doesn't necessarily mean she knew her."

"My gut instinct tells me otherwise. But that's not all. I found this newspaper article on Bevvie. And guess what the title is? *Hunting Accident or Murder?*"

"Holy shit. We've stepped in it now."

"You're not kidding. Listen. *When Larson Clayton went looking for moose in the wilds of Montana, he never expected to be the first big game felled by a hunting rifle. Members of the hunting party claim his death was an accident. The hunters had scattered and nobody knows whose gun fired the fatal shot. The hunting party included Larson's ex-wife, Angie, his brother, Clint Clayton, June Mathiston and Bevvie Laton.*"

"The paper wouldn't put murder in the headlines unless they had some evidence."

"Here's the scary part. *An unidentified source says the day before the hunt, Larson Clayton broke off his engagement to Bevvie Laton. The accident is under investigation.*"

"What did they find out?"

"Ballistics matched the bullet to Bevvie's gun, but no charges were filed."

"I'll bet she killed Bubbles, and if she's on the lam, we'll never get that old geezer in the ground."

"Don't let Uncle Charlie hear you speaking ill of the dead."

"Aunt Ruby Nell called him a two-timing turd. And Daddy didn't say a word."

"Yeah, but that's Mama."

"I wonder if it has any bearing on this case."

"Mama exaggerates."

"Not always. We know he was probably doing Bubbles. There might be something else. Ask her what she knows."

"Okay. Did you find out anything else from Kevin?"

"He said he and his sister Mellie are planning a trip abroad."

"Those two could have been in cahoots. Don't you dare see him again, Lovie. If we don't crack this case soon, you and I are liable to end up fried. And I'm not talking deep fat."

I strap on my holster and drive back to my beauty parlor packing cold steel. I have a family to live for. A dog. Future children.

They won't get me without a fight.

Ordinarily I'd go straight to Mama's and pick up Elvis, but I'm already late for my first hair appointment (Leonora Moffett, of all people), so I call and tell her to bring him to Everlasting Monuments. This could be anywhere between eleven and three. Mama's not known for keeping regular hours.

Fortunately I don't have to worry that Leonora will have to stand around in the parking lot sweating to death. All my clients know where I keep the spare key, so if I'm late, they just go in and help themselves to some of Lovie's Prohibition punch. I keep it in the refrigerator at all times. You never know when there'll be an emergency or a celebration. And if events don't coincide with your thirst, you can just invent one.

I pull the Dodge Ram into Hair.Net's empty parking lot. For some strange reason, Leonora's late. In case that reason is Jack, I fortify myself with Lovie's punch.

Mama says Leonora's nothing but a man-eating trollop, which would call for another glass of punch if I weren't the kind of woman who prides herself on knowing her limits.

Except maybe with shoes. And stray cats. And stray dogs. And Jack.

Shoot, this could get depressing if I'd let it.

Fortunately, a loud fracas jolts me out of my disturbing contemplative mood. Unfortunately, it's coming from Mama's monument company.

I set my glass on the unused manicure table and race toward the front door, but about that time Leonora bustles in and plops herself in the chair.

189

I'm so busy looking out the window at Jack spinning into Mama's place on his Harley, I almost miss the hickey on Leonora's neck.

I don't even want to know. Instead I start brushing her out.

"Ouch!" she says.

"Sorry. Tangles."

While I brush, I'm torn between inquiring about her day (discreetly, of course) or trying to figure out what's going on at Mama's.

Mama wins. There's another vehicle parked off toward the back that I didn't see at first glance. A green pickup. Could it be the robber Fayrene told me about?

Leonora's prattling on about her beauty routine. Right in the middle of her recital about mud packs, Uncle Charlie peels into Mama's parking lot and races into the building.

This looks serious. I'm about to excuse myself and tear after him, when who should come out of Mama's office but Buck Witherspoon—with Jack and Uncle Charlie pressed against him like bookends.

Buck does a bunch of loud talking. Unfortunately I can't hear what he's saying over Leonora's diatribe on beauty. As if I'm not Mooreville's resident expert.

Uncle Charlie is telling Buck something in that quiet, earnest way of his. I've never heard him raise his voice, even when he caught Lovie and me in full-blown teenage rebellion behind the barn trying out cigarettes.

But I've also never seen that expression. He looks downright dangerous.

Buck Witherspoon climbs into his truck and heads out with Jack following on his Harley. Then Uncle Charlie goes back into Mama's office and hangs the CLOSED sign in the window.

I can't finish Leonora's hair fast enough. As soon as she's gone, I race to Everlasting Monuments and bang on the door. By the time it opens, I've envisioned Uncle Charlie passing smelling salts beneath her nose while Mama lies on her Naughahyde couch, robbed and traumatized.

Mama, herself, swings open the door, and what do I see but a margarita in one hand and a cigarette in the other? To top it off, 'forties swing music blares from the stereo and my dog is dancing around imitating Bugsy Seagal entertaining a gun moll.

"Holy cow, Mama." It's all I can say. Obviously, sympathy is not in order here. "I didn't know you smoked."

"It's part of my secret life." She laughs like it's a big joke, but I have a sinking feeling she's not kidding. "Come on in and join the party."

"I thought you'd been robbed."

"It'll be a cold day in the tropics before I'll be anybody's victim. Ask Charlie."

"Your mother's a courageous woman."

"What happened?" I ask.

"A little disagreement, dear heart. It's all taken care of."

"What was Buck Witherspoon doing here?"

"You'll have to ask your mother."

"I'll never tell," Mama says, and I know it's useless to pry.

She proceeds to mix herself another drink and act like nothing's happened, which ought to make me feel better, but does just the opposite. If I hadn't already perked myself up with cute shoes and Lovie's Prohibition punch, I'd be ready for a straitjacket.

Plus, Uncle Charlie's gauging every move Mama makes. Like she's a piece of breakable china. Or a time bomb about to explode.

Finally he says, "Callie, I think it would be a good idea for you to spend the night with your mother."

It's the best idea I've heard all day. Delayed remorse over my foray into forbidden fornication has set in, and staying with Mama is one sure way to keep Jack from breaking and entering.

As nonchalant as Mama's acting, I expect her to protest that she doesn't need a caretaker, but she says, "If we're going to have a pajama party, let's invite Lovie."

Uncle Charlie kisses both of us. "You girls have fun tonight."

He grabs his hat and is at the door when Mama says, "Wait. Come, eat with us."

"I need to make sure Leonard's corpse stays put."

"Charlie, even God took one day to rest."

Finally he grins and says, "Okay." When he walks out there's a jauntiness about him that I haven't seen since this Laton business started.

Sometimes I'm so proud of Mama I could give her a crown.

After dinner, most of which Lovie cooked, Mama plays Broadway show tunes on the piano while she and Lovie and I sing. The way Uncle Charlie cheers, you'd think we were performing in Carnegie Hall. You'd think we weren't up to our necks in wandering corpses, frozen stiffs, death threats, and murder.

Elvis is looking peeved that he's not the center of the show, so I request "Hardheaded Woman," one of the King's big hits.

"My theme song." Mama begins belting it out while my dog perks up and howls along.

Listen, I know your typical American family does not spend their evenings singing with a dog, especially while mayhem reigns, but if I wanted to be typical I'd run away and put myself up for adoption with a family of bankers.

Later that evening while we're undressing for bed, Lovie spies my gun.

"When did you become a pistol-packing mama?"

"When Jack strapped on the leg holster."

Sometimes Lovie can look at you like she has inside information from God. I get the shivers standing there under her intense scrutiny. "What? *What?*"

"Callie, are you sure this divorce is the right thing?"

How can you ever be sure of anything? How can you know before the fact what consequences your actions will bring?

Can two hurting people knit together the torn fabric of a marriage and emerge with a whole cloth that is somehow stronger and better? If I knew the answer to that, I'd be President of Somewhere Important. I'd live on a mountaintop and people would make pilgrimages to hear me speak.

"I don't know, Lovie."

One of the many reasons I adore her is that she doesn't press. Instead, she pulls on a nightshirt that says *Do I Look Like I Care?* which is the exact opposite of the truth.

"We forgot to ask Aunt Ruby Nell about Dr. Laton."

"I didn't forget. I didn't want to ruin the evening." I also didn't forget about the newspaper articles burning a hole in my purse. I just wanted one evening of *normal.*

"Yeah, I know what you mean. Evenings like this make you feel innocent, don't they?" Lovie crawls into the bottom bunk. "Night, Callie."

The Valentine farm has always wielded that sort of magic.

Too full to speak, I climb the ladder and lie down in the top bunk. I've always felt safe up here—and powerful, capable of great things, poised for flight. I guess that's why I never got rid of the bunk beds even when my legs grew so long they touched the end of the footboard.

Plus, Mama's house is small and the stacked beds save space.

She added a skylight after Daddy died. I think it was because she knew I believed he had become a star. Now I pick him out in the sky and make a wish, partially for myself but mostly for Lovie.

"Whatever happens, let us keep the magic."

Elvis' Opinion # 8 on
Secrets, Striptease, and Cigarettes

This is the way it ought to be—me curled up on a rug with my belly full of leftover meat loaf while Callie and Lovie dream the innocent dreams of youth. Ruby Nell gave me the extra treat while Callie wasn't looking. Now, there's a woman who knows how to treat me nice.

If it hadn't been for me, Buck Witherspoon might have had his claws in her again, and she knows it. She even got Bunny for me to sleep with. Now, I like a rabbit as well as the next hound dog, even if it is stuffed. But if Ruby Nell had really wanted to show her appreciation she'd have opened the back door so I could trot down the street and spend some quality time with my little Frenchie.

What'd I say? I'm just a hunk a' burnin' love. But Ruby Nell's only human.

Actually, she's more human than most. That woman's full of juicy secrets.

When Buck Witherspoon slithered into Everlasting Monuments this afternoon looking like a snake oil salesman peddling a fresh batch, I plopped myself at Ruby Nell's feet and dared him to cross the line. Every quivering muscle in my body said, I'm so bad.

Not that Ruby Nell needed my help.

She grabbed a shotgun from the closet and said, "If you take one more step you're going to find your ugly self full of buckshot."

About that time Jack burst through the door with Charlie not far behind. And that's when things really got interesting.

"I'm fixing to spill the beans," Buck said.

Charlie had him by the throat and backed up against the wall so fast it didn't take a rocket scientist to figure out that the Valentine godfather's been in his share of barroom brawls.

Jack was standing there like a well-oiled killing machine, and of course, so was I. But I have sense enough to back off when another man's pride is involved, so I reined in my macho instincts and let Charlie be the hero.

The upshot of the fracas was that Jack escorted Buck to the sheriff's office where he'll be charged with a list of crimes in Lee County as long as my leg, including breaking and entering and harassment. After that he'll be extradited across state lines and handed over to the Alabama authorities, where he's wanted for grand theft, auto.

Of course, the juicy part of the story is what he was doing at Ruby Nell's.

Seems she's got a checkered past. It turns out she didn't take up gambling after Callie's daddy died: she took it up long before she met him. On the sly, of course. Back in her day, girls didn't smoke and gamble. And if they did, they earned reputations that made them outcasts of society.

Charlie knew about Ruby Nell's unladylike habits, but his brother was blinded by love. And so was Ruby Nell. After she met Michael Valentine, she was so smitten that she even tried to reform, but it didn't take.

I could have told her that. Reformation and strong wills don't gee haw. If I could have turned over a new leaf, I'd still be eating biscuits and sorghum molasses at the Delta Room in Chenault's up in Memphis.

Charlie has a way with cards, himself, so he took Ruby Nell under his wing and tried to keep her out of trouble. Then Buck Witherspoon entered the picture. Buck set sights on Ruby Nell the first time he ever saw her.

She and Charlie were at a card game up in Tishomingo County. He told Ruby Nell not to ever go without him, which was a waste of breath.

The next Saturday night she sneaked off without Charlie, and found herself on a losing streak playing five card stud. She was up to her pretty ears in debt.

She didn't have the cash to pay Buck and he said that was all right, she could work off the debt dating him. Well, she knew if she did that, her goose was cooked. There was no way word wouldn't get back to Michael Valentine, who was, by then, her fiancé.

So she made a devil's bargain. In exchange for forgiving the debt, Buck had Ruby Nell perform a private striptease. Nowadays, we'd call it a little lap dance.

Buck took her in the back room where she did a Gypsy Rose Lee imitation and stripped down to the bare essentials. Charlie thinks that meant her underwear, but knowing Buck—and Ruby Nell— I'd bet a good T-bone steak he's wrong. To get what she wants, it wouldn't faze Ruby Nell Valentine to show everything she's got (and she's got plenty).

She thought the score was settled; then after she was married, Buck showed up and started hanging around her, threatening to tell what she did if she wouldn't go out with him.

That's when Charlie stepped in and escorted Buck across the Alabama state line, all unbeknownst to Michael. I don't know what Charlie told Buck, but he must have been powerfully persuasive, because Buck didn't show his face on the farm again till this summer.

In my opinion, Ruby Nell's long-kept secret would no longer be a great scandal; it would just be another funny story to tell at cocktail parties.

But I'm a modern dog.

Charlie Valentine is from a different era, a gentleman who would challenge you to meet him at the dueling oaks in order to protect a woman's virtue.

Their secret's safe with me. Haven't I kept Jack's all these years?

Now, you may think I'm being disloyal to Callie, but trust me. If she knew everything about Jack and Ruby Nell, she'd only worry. She's better off staying in the dark.

And speaking of the dark, is that a sorry tomcat I hear yowling on Ruby Nell's back fence? Looks like I'm fixing to have to leave my beauty sleep and teach that alley cat a lesson.

I might not be able to get out the door, but I can create enough ruckus at the window to make him lose at least three of his nine lives. The last time I checked, I still had the vocals that turned every note out of my mouth to platinum and gold.

Chapter 15

Steam Heat, Rambo-ette, and Naked Truth

Grover Grimsley calls my cell phone in the middle of breakfast at Mama's. As much as I hate to leave country-fried ham and redeye gravy, I head into Tupelo with my gun and my canine bodyguard.

I picked a lawyer who loves dogs, so we shashay right in. It takes us a while to get down the hall to Grover's office because every person in the reception area has to pet Elvis and scratch behind his ears.

After we're seated, Grover gets right to the point.

"We could move this along much faster if you two could come to terms on custody. If your case has to go to court, it could take months. Even years if Jack wants to stall it that long."

I see my future unfold as an endless legal tangle while unborn babies get tired of waiting in the wings and move on to more fertile wombs.

"I'll see what I can do," I say, though I don't know of anything to change Jack's mind short of a miracle. "By the way, has anyone located Bevvie?"

"Not yet. There have been a few sightings—San Francisco, the Valley of Fire, the Grand Canyon. But she has a habit of disappearing."

Any one of those locations is near enough to Las Vegas that she could easily have killed Bubbles. Still, as closely as Uncle Charlie has watched the casket, wouldn't he have noticed if Bevvie showed up to restore her daddy's body? And even if Bevvie did it, that still leaves the mystery of the big man in the blood-colored truck.

This whole affair is getting depressing. I wish I had a habit I could fall back on that didn't cost money. Even collecting strays is costing me more than a closet full of Jimmy Choo shoes.

When I leave Grover's office, I'm greeted by a blast of hot, humid air as oppressing as his news. If I weren't wearing sassy Prada sling-back heels I could let it get me down.

I'd head straight to Lovie's for sympathy and chocolate, but I have appointments waiting at Hair.Net, and she has a retirement luncheon at Bancorp South. She had plans to leave Mama's right after breakfast to start cooking.

I do the next best thing, which is call her. Listen, women know about trouble. We understand adversity. When something threatens one of us, the rest circle around with souls anchored and hearts fierce. Like female elephants. When one of their number falls, they even weep.

See? Women also understand the beauty and healing of tears.

When Lovie answers, I tell her everything, including that the elusive Bevvie is still at large.

Miraculously, she proposes we meet this evening at the fitness center to sweat off our troubles.

"I thought you'd suggest chocolate."

"I'm on a diet."

"Great. What brought that on?"

"Champ."

I was hoping she'd say *self-motivation,* but after years of trying to get her to diet, I'm happy with what I can get.

Next I call Mama to see if Buck Witherspoon has materialized in her pasture, bent on mischief.

"He's in jail," she tells me. "Jack's here, just in case."

"Mama, did you call him?"

"Now, why would I do that?" As if she doesn't meddle in my life on a regular basis. "He came by of his own free will, thank you very much."

Sometimes Mama sounds the way Elvis looks, as sassy as a jaybird in a berry patch.

"Let me talk to him, please."

"Good."

"Mama, it's not what you think."

After Jack gets on the phone I try to talk some sense into him about letting me have full custody of Elvis.

"After all, you gave him to me. That makes him mine. You can visit whenever you like." That sounds like an invitation, like I want Jack Jones popping in and out of my life whenever he takes a notion. "As long as you call first."

His answer is a curt *no*. Next I try talking to him about freedom and how we both need to get on with our lives. I might as well be talking to a cypress knee.

As a result of this conversation I'm not my usual perky self when I walk into Hair.Net. When the office phone rings and I snarl out, "Hello," Elvis tucks his tail and hides under my desk.

"Callie Valentine?" I don't who this voice belongs to, but I wish I did. This is sexy George Clooney and reassuring Tom Brokaw all rolled up with the glory of the archangel Michael. This voice sounds like something I'd like to wrap around myself and cuddle up in.

"Yes, this is she," I say, formerly a telephone witch transformed into something that would melt in your mouth.

"I'm Luke Champion." Goodness gracious. Champ. No wonder Lovie's swapped chocolate for sweat. "I'm calling to check on Elvis."

"He's doing great." I don't tell him that he's pouting.

"Good. Let me know if you have any problems." He gives me his number, and after we hang up I wish I'd thought to ask if I need to bring Elvis in for a checkup. Just in case. Which just goes to show the length a woman with shriveling eggs will go to when she hears a voice with daddy potential.

Of course I would never do anything to interfere with Lovie's plans. She saw him first.

• • •

After six haircuts, two perms, and an unsolicited visit from Jack on my lunch break that ended up with me backed against the sink with my dress over my head, I'm more than ready to work off my frustrations at the fitness center. Listen, if it weren't for my certainty that Jack would never let me go and I'm not so sure I trust his wanderlust genes, I'd ditch the birth control pills and just go about this baby business all by myself.

Thank goodness I never forget to take them because my mind's made of steel (well, most of the time), even if my willpower's not.

Fayrene and Mama have plans tonight, which I sincerely hope do not include poker chips, so I drop Elvis off to keep Uncle Charlie company. Poor old Gertrude's wake is tonight, and Elvis has a way of cheering up the bereaved. In fact, we pride ourselves on being the only funeral home in Tupelo that offers the comfort of a famous dog.

Over a cup of coffee, Uncle Charlie reports that Dr. Laton is still in his chain-bound coffin and no new gifts have been placed on his chest.

As I head back to my car, I notice the red Ford F-150 lurking in the parking lot, half hidden by a magnolia tree. Racing back inside, I discreetly pull Uncle Charlie aside.

"The intruder's back."

"Wait right here."

"What are you going to do? Call the police?"

"Take care of this."

He heads toward the back door, but I'm not about to stand by while he gets himself killed. One body in the freezer is enough. Besides, I'm the one with the gun.

I ease out the door and spot Uncle Charlie hiding behind a Buick sedan a few feet from the red pickup. Unholstering my gun, I crouch low and move toward the Buick. Vigilante justice in high heels.

A stray pebble waylays me, and I go down. Hard. My gun discharges and blows a hole in the sky. Suddenly Uncle Charlie's on the run and the Ford F-150 barrels toward me, the beams on his roll bar lighting me up like a Macy's Day Parade Christmas tree. I'm fixing to be flattened like a frog. The only good thing I can say is that I'm already at the funeral home.

Staring at my own face in the cold metal bumper while my life flashes before me, I try to think sacred thoughts, but all that comes to mind is the credit card bill I owe at Lucky's Shoes.

Suddenly Uncle Charlie leaps in front of the Ford and scoops me out of the way.

"Are you all right, dear heart?"

"I'm fine." I stand up, shaky, lopsided, and *alive*, and then I spot the victim—one of my Prada shoes. Even my hot glue gun won't fix it. I try not to mourn. There are greater things at stake here than fashion. "I'm sorry, Uncle Charlie. I blew it." Stealth and high heels don't mix.

People pour out of the funeral home, asking what happened. Uncle Charlie pockets my gun so fast I barely see his hands move.

"Somebody shot off firecrackers," he tells the crowd. "Everything's under control."

After the gawkers disperse, we head up the back stairs to Uncle Charlie's apartment. We have no qualms about leaving Elvis in charge downstairs. I've never seen an audience my dog couldn't charm.

"Sit down and relax, dear heart. I'll call Dr. Jones."

"No. I'm fine. Really. I'm just so sorry I messed things up. You almost had him."

"I got his tag number."

This is the first break we've had in the moveable corpse case. I can't wait to tell Lovie. Uncle Charlie insists I take his car and leave in disguise in case the man in the Ford F-150 is watching.

Fifteen minutes later I slip out of the funeral home dressed in a pair of ballerina flats Lovie left behind and Uncle Charlie's overalls with my hair tucked under his felt fedora. I nab my gym bag from the Dodge Ram, then drive with my eyes peeled on the rearview mirror. Under the distorting glare of streetlights, every approaching vehicle looks like a Ford truck. Bloodred.

Lovie's waiting for me. In a bikini swimsuit.

Neon orange with big glow-in-the-dark Hawaiian flowers. I'm glad she decided to meet me in the dressing room instead of the parking lot.

"Good grief, Callie. Are those my shoes? What's going on?"

Four women in designer exercise togs who ought to be spending some of their money on good haircuts stare at us, all ears. I shake my head at Lovie, then open my gym bag and pull out my jogging shoes.

"Are you going to ride the stationary bicycle in that outfit?" I ask.

"Silly you. Who said anything about riding a bicycle? I thought we'd sweat the easy way. In the sauna."

Sitting down will be a relief, even if it is the dreaded sauna. Ducking behind the curtains into a tiny dressing area, I start shucking my clothes. I never darken the sauna doors unless Lovie's along for company. If I'm going to sweat I want it to have some lofty purpose—like tending roses or tending the libido. Listen, if God hadn't meant for people to enjoy sex, he'd have given Adam and Eve something to wear besides fig leaves.

Five minutes later we're sprawled on benches— Lovie in her swimsuit and me in a towel—while sweat the size of golf balls rolls off us. The only bright side I can see is that Lovie and I have been so bad this is good practice if we end up in perdition.

We have the sauna all to ourselves, so I tell her about the latest fracas with the Ford.

"Did your shots bring the cops?"

"No, thank goodness. If they had I'd be under arrest right now. Don't forget, we're the most likely suspects in Bubbles' murder."

Suddenly the door bursts open and I'm face-to-face with Bevvie Laton. She looks just like her picture—blond, brawny, and dangerous—and she dwarfs her sister, Mellie, who stands beside her like a pet mouse.

Lovie and I exchange a look that says, *I wonder if they heard.* We gravitate toward each other, safety in a united front.

"Do you mind if we join you?" Mellie asks, but Bevvie pushes her way inside before we can say anything. "Bevvie, this is Callie and Lovie. Valentine. You know. Of the funeral home family."

Mellie looks like she's going faint. I feel sorry for her.

"Sit down, Mellie." Bevvie towers in the doorway and glares at us. "What were you saying about Bubbles Malone?" No wonder she can kill Bambi's daddy without mercy. If I were that brassy I'd melt myself down and open a hardware store. "She stole every penny of Daddy's money. That gold digger deserves to die."

Lord have mercy. Did she say *deserves* or *deserved?* How long has she been eavesdropping and what else did she hear? More to the point, what's she hiding under that big towel besides a killer body? A knife?

"I think we've been in here our limit, Lovie."

I stand up, but Bevvie grabs my arm and jerks me back down.

"Sit. I'm not finished with you."

Lovie lurches like she's fixing to launch herself at Bevvie, wrestle her to the floor, and sit on her. I grab a handful of Hawaiian flowers and hold on. There's been enough bloodshed.

"Please, Bevvie. Don't start anything else. It's already bad enough." Mellie plucks her sister's arm, but Bevvie brushes her off.

"Now that I'm back, I want you to know there will be no more delays and no more shenanigans. Don't think I don't know about the red pasties. One more stunt like that, and I'll trounce your family in the courts so thoroughly you'll wish you were in the middle of a level-five hurricane."

Mellie bursts into tears and races out of the sauna.

"Now what?" Bevvie takes off after her.

"Thank goodness, that's over." I stand up and my wet, heavy towel slides to the floor. "Let's get out of here before I faint from this heat."

Lovie has already beat me to the door, and is pulling to no avail. "It's locked!" She pounds it with her fists while her swimsuit does the hula.

The heat feels as if it has been turned up twenty degrees. I wonder how long it will take us to dehydrate. Or will we broil to death first?

I pound on the door with Lovie, yelling for help.

"Nobody can hear us, Callie. We're going to die in here."

"Not without a fight." I try to sound confident instead of like a terrified woman who wishes she didn't have so many sins to repent before she dies. Scooping my towel off the floor, I wrap it around my right foot and leg.

"Have you gone mad? What are you doing?"

"Stand back, Lovie. I'm going to kick the door in."

I take a karate stance and lunge—right through the suddenly open door and into Fayrene. She screams as we crazy-dance across the room and plow into the opposite wall.

Before I launched myself, she was standing innocently outside the door in a swimsuit that was in style during the 'fifties when Esther Williams did movies featuring underwater ballet.

"Are you okay, Fayrene?"

"I will be if that blow to my head doesn't give me demetrius."

I must already have dementia. Otherwise, I'd have remembered to push the door from the inside, not pull.

"Do you want me to call a doctor?"

"Lord, no. I'm just going to go home and pour myself a big glass of sweet tea and stretch out on my new sexual sofa."

Translation, *sectional*. Unless Lane Furniture has something new I ought to know about.

"Is Mama with you?"

"She's at the funeral home. We went to the library for the lecture on flower arranging from that new florist in town, but his dysentery went on so long we got up and left. Is that a hickey on your neck?"

"Bug bite." I cover it with my hand. Drat Jack Jones' hide.

After we've assured ourselves that Fayrene is not injured, we escort her to her car and agree to meet at Uncle Charlie's. It's time for another family powwow.

Chapter 16

Rocky Times, Rock Bottom, and Rocky Malone

Lovie and I drive back to the funeral home bumper to bumper. If somebody's out to kill us, they'll have to take us both down at the same time.

On the way, I call to brief Uncle Charlie. By the time we arrive, he has steaming mugs of green tea chai and Mama has blankets, which she proceeds to bundle around us as if it's not still ninety degrees outside.

Funny thing is, cuddling inside a fuzzy blanket while Elvis snuggles beside me and the ten o'clock news plays in the background makes nearly getting killed twice in one evening seem like a bad dream. Judging by the way Lovie's hanging on to hers, I'd say she feels the same way.

Furthermore, Mama says, "You and Lovie are staying with me tonight, and don't argue."

That I'm willing to endure an evening of unsolicited marriage counseling and bad advice without protest proves I've hit rock bottom. Never mind the magical charm of the farm.

Reaching for my purse, I pull out copies of the newspaper pictures and hand them to Uncle Charlie.

"See what you make of these. You can see Bubbles Malone at Janice's party. Kevin knew her, too, but lied about it. Bevvie's already been suspected of murder. So far, the only Laton who didn't have a connection to Bubbles is Mellie."

"They all had motives for murdering Bubbles," Lovie says. "But ordinary people don't kill just because they get cut out of an inheritance. The killer had to be somebody who would benefit in some way from her death or somebody who hated her so much just seeing her dead was reward enough."

"Mama, what do you think? You said Dr. Laton was a playboy. Could he have done anything that would make one of his children want to kill Bubbles Malone?"

"Forget all that. We could hide out on one of those riverboats in Natchez while the police handle the homicide investigation." Naturally, she means *riverboat gambling*. It's not enough that I contribute heavily to the economy of Tunica; now Mama's planning to range southward. I draw the line at financing the resurrection of the once-notorious Natchez Under the Hill.

"Don't worry, dear heart. Jack's on the case."

"What does an international businessman know about catching a killer?" I'm more than flabbergasted; I'm curious.

"About as much as a hairdresser and a caterer, would be my guess," Lovie says, and I applaud while she gets up to refill everybody's cups. "Aunt Ruby Nell, you never did tell what you know about Dr. Laton."

"Everybody knew Leonard couldn't keep his pecker in his pants. His wife left him over it. Then she went back."

"When?" I ask.

"Before they adopted Kevin. For a while there was a rumor Kevin was his love child, but it fizzled out so fast nothing ever came of it."

"With Bubbles Malone?" I ask. "That would account for her bailing Kevin out of jail. But it would also make him less likely to be the killer. Or maybe, more likely. I think I've read there's often a close connection between killer and victim."

Uncle Charlie has been quiet up to this point. Now he defends his old friend.

"Leonard sowed a few wild oats when he was

young, but the man I knew and fished with would have claimed Kevin as his natural child if that were true. He would have wanted his son to know."

Lovie shushes us and goes over to turn up the volume on the TV.

"In the bizarre homicide case of the former strip dancer, Bubbles Malone, who was found dead in her chest freezer, Las Vegas police are following new leads that could result in an arrest."

The camera pans to Detective Rusty Satterfield, whose only comment is that in order not to compromise the case, the Las Vegas PD is keeping all details under wraps.

Lovie turns pale and I don't feel so hot, myself.

Uncle Charlie switches off the TV. "Let's talk about opportunity. Who was in Las Vegas at the time of the murder?"

With visions of jailhouse bread and water dancing in my head, I'm too shook-up to speak, and so is Lovie.

"We know the man in the red Ford was there, and Bevvie was in the area, too." Uncle Charlie turns to Mama. "Is it possible Janice could have made the trip without you noticing she was gone?"

"No way. My mind's a laser. I can sniff out people faster than Elvis. And I certainly never forget anything." She gives me this *look* that says *You went to Vegas without me and I'll carry it to my grave.*

"Wait a minute. There was that day Fayrene and I drove to Memphis shopping."

"What about Mellie?" Uncle Charlie asks. "Does anybody know her whereabouts on the day of the murder?"

"I do. Well, sort of. When Lovie and I got back, Kevin said she'd been holed up in her house. Janice was mad because she wouldn't take her calls. Plus, we saw her at Kevin's."

"Yeah," Lovie says. "Talking about murder."

"That takes us back to why?" I get up and stare at the picture of Mellie and the escort whose face still makes the hair on the back of my neck stand on end. "The man in the red Ford is trying to kill us, but why would he kill Bubbles? What's his connection?"

When the phone rings, Uncle Charlie goes into the hall to answer it, and Mama goes right after him, never mind that his private phone calls are none of her business.

"Do you think the Las Vegas police know we were there?" I ask Lovie.

"Half the city knows we were asking about her. Besides, Marsha saw us when we visited that afternoon."

"Yeah, but she thinks we're from Minnesota."

Mama prisses back in and sits down. "It's Jack."

"What does he want?" I'm getting a little anxious that my almost-ex pops up every time I need him. And believe me, I would willingly fall off the redemption wagon for a few hours of forgetfulness. Is the universe trying to tell me something?

"That was Jack," Uncle Charlie says, as if we don't already know. "He ran the tag number on the red Ford. It belongs to Rocky Malone."

My first question is, how on earth did Jack Jones do something that can't be done? Your ordinary Tom, Dick, and Harriet can't just march to a computer and Google confidential stuff like tag numbers. That's for police and FBI and CIA and a bunch of other initials I never heard of. And don't tell me I don't know the man I've been sleeping with. My ex doesn't have what it takes to ensure world peace. He couldn't even ensure peace in his own home.

"Is he related to Bubbles?" Lovie shucks off her blanket and grabs a handful of Hershey's Kisses from a blue bowl on the coffee table.

"I don't know," Uncle Charlie says. "So far all Jack has is that Rocky was once arrested for disorderly conduct at a nightclub called Hot Tips. Jack's going to track it down."

My almost-ex again. *See,* I knew there was a reason I can't trust that man. Apparently he has this whole other secret life that allows him direct connection to the underbelly of society. Plus, if he keeps digging around he's going to find out about my questionable activities at Hot Tips. This makes me so mad I want to hit him with my Jimmy Choos.

I'm getting tired of Jack acting as if I can't take care of myself, coming and going as he pleases, picking locks and entering at will. I'm determined to prove that I can not only function brilliantly without him, but I can solve this homicide.

"What we ought to do is question the people who knew the suspects," I say.

"Brilliant, Sherlock Holmes. We had so much luck the last time." Lovie tosses me a Hershey's Kiss.

I ignore her jab. "Thank you, Dr. Watson."

"We don't have much time," Uncle Charlie says. "Now that Bevvie's back, we're going to finally get Leonard in the ground."

"Who says he'll stay?" Mama asks.

"I've put a string of garlic under him, just in case," Uncle Charlie says, deadpan, and he and Mama crack up.

I imagine he's joking about the garlic, but lately I've decided there are things about him I can't even begin to guess. It's just good to see him laughing.

On the way to Mooreville, Lovie and I stop by her house for some clothes. I bail out of my Dodge Ram, but I never can keep up with Lovie. Before I have finished telling Elvis "I'll be right back," she's at her front door, yelling.

"Callie, quick!"

I jerk out my gun and make sure the safety is on. The way my luck has been running, I can't be too careful, and Lovie would be less than happy if I shot off one of her prized body parts.

Taking the steps two at a time, I'm going so fast I ram into her. She explodes with a heartfelt string of words I hope my dog doesn't hear. He has enough bad habits without taking up howling words that would scandalize the Baptist church ladies.

"What's wrong?" I ask.

"Take a look." Lovie holds up the latest threat— a pair of red pasties, sparkling under the glow of front porch lights. "If that fool's going to keep leaving these, the least he could do is get some in my size."

"Where'd you get those?"

"Pinned to this."

Lovie hands me a note scrawled in dripping red. The words send chills and nightmares of lying in Lovie's camellia bush with my throat slit: *I saw what you did.*

"Is it blood?" I ask.

"No. Hunt's catsup."

"How do you know?"

"My nose is so refined I could sniff out truffles."

"Let's leave, Lovie. Forget about clothes. This Rocky Malone character could be inside."

"I'm not convinced he's the red pasties perpetrator." Lovie picks up a flowerpot, planted. "I'm not letting anybody keep me out of my house."

We ease open the door and sneak inside, me in

front gripping the gun and Lovie behind me, hefting the pot and trailing pink wave petunias.

"Come get me, sucker," she yells.

"Shhh. What if he hears us?"

"That's the idea. When I took Tan Sui karate, my grand master said *never let anybody smell your fear.*"

"I didn't know you took karate."

"You were in Atlanta. My hands are lethal weapons. Ask any one of my old boyfriends."

If we're going to die tonight, we might as well die laughing.

Elvis' Opinion # 9 on Bodyguards, Uneven Ears, and Four-Letter Words

Lovie has a colorful way with language, and Callie's probably cringing that I'm in the truck listening. Take it from me; I'm a dog of world. In my heyday I used a word or two myself. But when you've been around a lifetime or two, you get a little wiser, a little more mellow. Nowadays, my favorite four-letter *F* word is *fame.*

If they'd put me on the job, I could reclaim my fame—this time around as the most renowned dog detective in the world. I have my ways. I know things. For instance, even if I hadn't overheard Callie and Lovie talking, I could tell you without looking what's in that note.

It's a threat—just like the one Jack found on the door of Callie's beauty shop.

If Ruby Nell had stuck around when Jack called Charlie tonight, she'd know, too. But she's too impatient. Has to be running and doing, always thinking she's in the know. Let me tell you, it takes the precision of a stakeout artist to get the inside scoop. That and a set of radar ears.

Don't let the uneven nature of mine fool you. I can hear Jack's Harley coming for miles. Overhearing both ends of a telephone conversation is nothing to a dog of my talents.

But back to Callie's note . . . It said *Crime does not pay.* Of course, she'll never see it. Jack made sure of that. He's having it analyzed for finger-prints, which is more than I can say for Lovie's note. The way those two are mauling it, there won't be a single, usable print left.

They're headed into the house now. If I didn't know what I know, I'd break out of this truck in a New York minute and be in there throwing my weight around. But I know something they don't know: Jack's watching. Charlie asked him to make sure *the girls* were okay, but Jack would have been on the job, regardless. You don't mess with what's his, and he considers Callie his.

Of course, what she considers is a different thing, but I have too much on my mind to get into marriage counseling.

Lovie and Callie will never know he's trailing them: Jack's got more stealth than the stealth bomber. But like I said, I can hear that Harley for miles. Which bodes well for me. With a little help from Jack, I can sneak out of the house tonight and have a go at that dratted tomcat. Furthermore, I can spend some quality time howling at the moon.

Here comes Callie, waving and calling me *sweet pea* and *baby.*

Back to my role as favorite pet.

Chapter 17

Uninvited Guests, Loose Tongues, and Loose Libidos

Jack's Screamin' Eagle wakes me from a sound sleep, and I sit up so fast I nearly tumble out of the top bunk. Lovie's snoring in the bottom bunk and Elvis is snoring on the rug, which means I must be dreaming. If Jack were anywhere within five miles, Elvis would be at the window wagging his tail.

I climb down and grab my robe anyway because Mama's in the kitchen brewing coffee and frying bacon. Elvis doesn't stir.

Holy cow. Is he dead? I call his name, but he just opens one eye then goes right back to sleep.

In the kitchen I grab a piece of bacon, then go back in the bedroom and wave it around. It brings Elvis and Lovie both to life.

"Up and at 'em. We have sleuthing to do."

Lovie and I don't have much time for questioning friends of the suspects. Dr. Laton's funeral is tomorrow, and she's doing the Laton's food while I'm doing Janice's hair.

Leaving Elvis with Mama, we head out at the crack of eight in our latest disguise. We look like Billy Graham in drag. Navy blue linen suits, hair in tight buns, reading glasses perched on the nose, and orthopedic shoes Mama bought after her hip surgery. The only thing that could make me wear these ugly shoes is the threat of jail.

Our first visit is to Kevin's next door neighbor. We feel safe here because Lovie knows he'll be at work. Besides, his car is gone.

I punch the buzzer and a woman in a short robe that shows sagging legs and knobby knees comes to the door. Her gray hair is wadded up in brush rollers, and pink plastic picks are sticking out all over her head. I have to bite my tongue to keep from telling her those things will split her ends.

"Hi," Lovie shouts, and the woman jumps back three feet. "We're with the Ever Blooming Garden Club, and we're getting ready to nominate your next door neighbor as Tupelo's Citizen of the Year."

"Kevin? My, my, isn't that nice?"

"Oh yes," I say. "It's quite an honor. But we need your help. Do you mind if we ask you a few questions?"

"He'll be back around four. I'm sure he can tell you more about himself than I can."

"I'm sure," Lovie says. "But the nominations are secret. You've read about it in the paper, of course. Part of the fun is catching the winner by surprise."

The woman holds her door open. "As long as they spell my name right in the paper. That's Sugarbee Martindale, one word spelled with two *es*. My mama said I was born due to the birds and the bees and I was just as sweet as pie."

Perched on the edge of her oversized recliner, Sugarbee looks like a sparrow as she pulls her robe shut where it has gaped to show her pink nylon gown. "Now, what do ya'll want to know? I've got all day."

"That's very nice of you," I say, and when Sugarbee launches into a blow-by-blow account of the beef and beans casserole she made to welcome Kevin to the neighborhood, Lovie kicks me under the coffee table.

"We're in kind of a rush," I say. "This form has to be turned in by ten. His coworkers told us Kevin's dedicated to his job. Do you concur?"

"I don't know so much about that, but I'd say he leaves here every morning at seven thirty like clockwork. Unless he's sick."

When Lovie asks, "Has he been sick lately?" I feel certain Sugarbee will smell a rat and show us the door. But she chirps on, obviously happy at the prospect of getting her name in the paper.

"He was out with a bug last week. Sick as a dog, he told me later. Why, he couldn't even come to the door when I carried him some chicken soup. And it was my aunt Matilda's recipe."

We pin her down, and sure enough, Kevin "couldn't even come to the door" about the time Bubbles Malone was being killed and frozen like corn-fed veal.

We're getting ready to dig deeper when Sugarbee's doorbell chimes—and in walks one of Tupelo's finest, complete with a cocaine-sniffing dog. Sugarbee greets him in the hall and he calls her *Mom,* but Lovie and I don't stick around to find out the purpose of his visit. In case it's us, we hightail it through the kitchen and toward the back door so fast I leave one of my orthopedic shoes behind.

Lovie backtracks and snatches it up just as Sugarbee is saying, "Now, where in the world did they go?"

"To catch our coach before it turns to a pumpkin." Safely outside I feel free to make wisecracks, but Lovie doesn't hear me. She's pulled ahead by two lengths. By the time I catch her, she has grabbed my spare key from the magnetic box under the chassis and already has the motor running.

"Hurry." She tosses me the shoe. "Hang on to that, Cinderella. The man in blue's not a prince and you can bet your thong he's not fixing to propose marriage."

Something with bars is more like it. I put on my ugly shoe and act like this doesn't faze me. "Where to next?"

"Somewhere dark. And safe. The back of my closet?"

"With the Las Vegas police following clues that are bound to lead to us?"

"Officer Jenkins was kind of cute."

"You'll think *cute* when we land in jail. Besides, it'll take more than flirting to get us out of this mess. Turn right." She starts cutting left, and I yell, "*Right*, Lovie."

"Where are we going?"

I can't answer immediately; I'm too busy trying to breathe. Lovie corrected the van in mid-turn and almost straddled the light pole on the corner of Jefferson and Main.

"The old white house west of the library."

Lovie pulls into a narrow lane that meanders behind a two-story white-clapboard house that has been turned into apartments. It looks like the kind of place a timid woman would choose, quaint and quiet, all the books she wants only a short walk from her door.

I've seen Mellie at the guest lectures during National Library Week, always dressed in unstylish clothes in somber colors, always alone. I imagine her spending evenings in the library reading Jane Austen, surrounded by people and yet safely tucked into a corner where she's almost invisible.

We get out of the van and check for a lurking Ford F-150 while we adjust our severe skirts and tacky buns.

"What if she sees us, Callie?"

"She's probably at work."

"What does she do?"

"How should I know?"

"You could've just asked Janice. She was right there in your house."

"Did you ever ask Kevin?"

"There's no need to get your thong in a wad, Callie."

She knows me too well. I *am* wearing a thong. Just in case. I priss straight to the first door I see and give it a whack.

Who should answer my knock but Mellie Laton?

"Yes?" she says. "Can I help you?"

I can tell she doesn't recognize me. She looks like we just woke her from a nap. And besides, she's not wearing her glasses.

"Run," Lovie's hissing in my ear like a tire with a slow leak.

"Did somebody say *run?*"

"There's a run in Lovie's stocking. We just stopped by to see if you're okay." I whip off my glasses and Lovie does the same.

"Oh yes, the sauna. I had a bit of a stomachache, but I've fully recovered." Grabbing my hand, Mellie tugs me inside with a grip that is surprisingly strong. "Come in. I was getting ready to make tea."

"We can't." Lovie's planted in the threshold like General Custer at Little Big Horn.

Mellie surges forward, dragging me in her wake. Finally Lovie surrenders her position and plops into a chair nearest the door. Thank goodness, Mellie doesn't lock it behind us.

Gathering my last wit, I examine the apartment. She's certainly not neat, but I was right about the library books. They're everywhere—piled on the coffee table, spilling onto the floor from woven baskets, scattered on the sofa and the side tables. Nobody can read that fast. I'll bet she owes her soul in overdue fees.

I give her a black mark. Everybody can forget an occasional book, but anybody who checks out that many books and doesn't return them will do no telling what.

Including murder?

"Are you cold?" Mellie puts on her glasses, then just stares.

"A little. I must be coming down with the same thing you had at the sauna."

Mellie's still staring. "I like your suit."

Is she serious or is she on to us? "Thanks. We've been to a board meeting."

"Why don't I get us some tea?" She scurries off, her ugly brown rubber-soled shoes hardly making a sound.

Mellie could sneak up behind you, and you'd never hear her. And I don't even have my gun. It's in my old bedroom at Mama's on the dresser. After shooting up the parking lot at Eternal Rest and nearly shooting Lovie on her front porch, I figured I'd be better off without it. Now I'm not so sure.

"There's two of us." Lovie has an uncanny ability to read my mind.

"Just act natural. And unbutton your jacket. We'll be fine."

In spite of current circumstances, I believe that. I've survived the premature death of my daddy and the death of my marriage, not to mention the untimely demise of one of my best Prada shoes. Not only survived, but triumphed—if you count having the best little beauty parlor in Lee County and the best show dog in the state. And I do, even though Elvis has never won a single award.

We'll keep trying. Life's never going to be perfect. Just jut out your chin and keep forging forward. That's my motto.

Actually, one of my many. I pride myself on being a multifaceted woman.

By the time Mellie returns with three thin porcelain cups of tea, I feel up to any challenge. Even solving a homicide.

I take a sip, belatedly wishing I'd just pretended in case it's poisoned, then put on my best company smile.

"So, Mellie. Everything is all set for the funeral tomorrow. I'm sure this has been an ordeal for you."

"I've managed."

"How?" Lovie asks.

I shoot her a look, then sail into a soliloquy about the value of good friends in time of trouble. Shakespeare must be rolling in his grave.

While I'm pontificating, Lovie asks for directions to the bathroom, then huffs off.

"Not many people drop by," Mellie says, and I tell her, "We should have called first."

"No. I'm always here."

"Are you retired?"

"I work out of my apartment. I do billing and accounts for several doctors in town."

"How nice to have that kind of freedom. Personally, I like being my own boss. I can come and go as I please." I sip my tea, which is really delicious. Obviously it's not poisoned or I'd be facedown on the floor by now.

Lovie comes back and sits there with her eyebrows bouncing up and down and her eyes twitching. She's either trying to signal me or developing a strange malady.

"In fact, Lovie and I took a little trip last week. Out West."

Mellie blanches and Lovie's eyebrows shoot into her hairline. She gives me a look that says *have you lost your mind?*

"Out West?" Mellie sets her cup down.

"Sightseeing," I tell her. "Mostly camping in the Valley of Fire."

Let Mellie mull over that a while. If she's guilty of anything, knowing we were in Vegas might be enough to flush her out.

When we're back in the van Lovie says, "Are you crazy? What if she's the killer?"

"We're twice Mellie's weight and three times her height. We could have whipped her with one hand tied behind our backs."

"Guns are a great equalizer, Callie."

"Mellie's not the kind to have weapons."

"You didn't see that double-barreled twelve-gauge shotgun in her bathroom closet."

"Holy cow. Did you notice how fast Mellie developed a headache and showed us the door when I mentioned our trip?"

"You would, too, if Bubbles Malone had stolen your daddy's money."

"Which leave us right back where we started. All the Latons had motive and opportunity. Probably means, too, since we don't know the murder weapon."

"Next time we find a corpse in the freezer, you should look and find out, Callie."

"After this is over, the only corpses I plan to see up close and personal are the well-behaved deceased at Uncle Charlie's funeral home."

Lovie and I return to the farm to change clothes and redo our hair. I'd go without mascara before I'd let my customers see me in these tacky shoes.

She heads back to Tupelo and I call Mama's cell phone to locate my dog.

"We're at Fayrene's store," she says.

I'm not even going to ask. Last year Fayrene converted a stockroom at the back of her store by adding green curtains and a 1950s dinette set with a pink Formica top and pink vinyl seat cushions. She calls it a break room, but I have my doubts. For one thing, she keeps quarters in the middle of her table in a Mason jar. For another, after Mama's trips across the road for a "cuppa java" with Fayrene, her purse rattles.

After perking myself up with fluffy hair and a pair of hot-pink Taryn Rose sling-backs, I head to Gas, Grits, and Guts to get my dog.

This is not as easy as it sounds. Today's Friday, flea market day. Vendors vie for space on the small lot with dealers selling antiques and junk out of the tailgates of their pickups. I squeeze my Dodge Ram into a spot behind the boiled peanut stand, and the first person I see is Janice. She and her brood are crowded around Dick Newsome, aka the knife man.

I don't want her to know I see her fondling a hunting knife with a blade mean enough to gut a fattening hog. I'm getting ready to duck my head and race inside when I spot Elvis lifting his leg on the knife man's tires.

Forget anonymity. This is my dog we're talking about. As I skirt eastward to the rescue, who should I run into but Mama? She puts her fingers to her lips and motions to me.

Hunkering down beside her on the other side of the pickup, I ask, "What are you doing?"

"Spying on Janice."

"Good grief, Mama."

"Keep your voice down. I'm incognito."

She's wearing a red straw hat big enough to shade both of us, Jackie O sunglasses with rhinestones, and a neon-yellow caftan you can see to the county line. People are already staring. Pretty soon, they'll be lining up for autographs.

"Come on, Mama. Let's go."

We sprint toward my Dodge Ram, then head to Hair.Net, where Mama proceeds to help herself to my Inferno Red nail polish while Elvis puts his nose to the floor and checks the place for intruders (or maybe dropped potato chips). I go into my office to check messages. There are four asking for appointments and one from Janice canceling hers. Thank goodness. If I ever got her in my chair I'd probably pull her hair out. For general aggravation, if nothing else.

The last message is from Lovie's latest heartthrob saying he'd like to check Elvis in a follow-up appointment.

"Who was that?" Mama's standing in the door making no bones about eavesdropping on stuff that is none of her business. When I tell her about the new vet, she says, "Have you seen Jack?"

Mama's so predictable.

"Not today."

"Well, you ought to make a point. Considering the dangerous riffraff he's handling for us, you could soon be a widow. Black's not your color."

I'm not fixing to get tangled up in another of Mama's windy dissertations about holding your man.

"Did you learn anything new about Janice, Mama?"

"It seems Bevvie's not the only family member who kills for sport. Janice hunts with a bow and arrow. So does her husband. For all we know, they could be Bonnie and Clyde."

"But they were in Mooreville when Bubbles was killed."

"Not necessarily. You know that little side trip I took? To Memphis? Well, it turns out Janice made a flying trip to the West Coast and took the red-eye back."

"Why?"

"Supposedly to check on a sick friend. But I don't trust anybody who's had that much plastic surgery."

"What does that have to do with anything, Mama?"

"If you're fool enough to have your face lifted off, you're fool enough to do anything."

I tend to agree. Give me what God and Estee Lauder intended.

Mama heads back to Everlasting Monuments while Trixie Moffett (evil Leonora's good cousin) arrives for highlights and advice on her disappointing love life. I'd be disappointed, too, if I had to depend on Roy Jessup at Mooreville Feed and

Seed for my sexual excitement. I recommend high-heel shoes and Jungle Gardenia perfume, then end up giving her the hot-pink Taryn Rose sling-backs right off my feet.

I spend the rest of the afternoon doing hair in my bare feet, which is normal for me. After the last customer leaves, Mama calls in a triumphant dither to report that somebody drove all the way from Red Bay, Alabama, to buy a monument engraved *If I send postcards from the other side, you'll know.*

Uncle Charlie also calls to say the last remains of Durell Thompson have been delivered to Eternal Rest but the funeral's delayed pending the arrival of family from Wisconsin.

"I'm glad. I don't do my best work when I'm nervous."

"Take a break, dear heart. There's no need for you and Lovie to attend Dr. Laton's public viewing tonight. You've been through enough. Relax and enjoy the evening."

With the California Latons at the funeral home, I put on my favorite blue summer lounging pajamas and ostrich-trimmed blue satin mules, then settle on my sofa for a leisurely evening watching movies with Elvis.

Viva Las Vegas is playing. In spite of Elvis' preference in movies, I'm not fixing to ruin my night with reminders. I'm flipping through channels looking for something else when I hear Bubbles' name on the six o'clock news.

Flipping back, I see a female reporter standing in front of the cottage on Cactus Lane, interviewing a skinny fiftyish woman wearing a blue top with a scarf that makes her neck look too short.

"In a bizarre twist to the case, LaBelle Clemmons' Pomeranian brought a nasty surprise to her door."

Oh my Lord. I grab my cell.

"Lovie, quick. Turn on Channel nine."

"Why?"

"Just listen."

The reporter holds the microphone in front of LaBelle.

"What did you do when your little dog brought the finger to your door?"

"Woke up my husband screaming."

"The Pomeranian's grizzly gift has been identified as the left pinky finger that once belonged to Bubbles Malone."

"Lovie, are you there?"

"I didn't know he chewed it off. Did you?"

"No. I was too busy trying to get her to bend."

"I don't want to go to jail."

"I never met anybody who did. Look on the bright side, Lovie. We didn't kill her."

"Yeah, but we're the ones who got her body parts chewed off. That's probably a crime."

"Pinkie theft? Appendage abduction?"

"You have lost your tiny mind."

She's probably right. I'm also about to lose my supper. Running into my hall bath, I sit on the cold tile floor hugging the toilet and heaving. Nothing comes up but the certainty that my evening is ruined.

I just hope my life's not.

Chapter 18

Cops, Clues, and Blue Christmas

Funeral day is always a big occasion for the Valentine family. We all dress up, even Elvis, who loves to wear his rhinestone-studded collar with the bow tie. Pink. His signature color. I'm wearing pink, too, and my sassiest Jimmy Choo open-toed pumps.

The Valentine family does not believe in dressing in black. Black's for mourning and there's nothing somber and mournful about funeral services at Eternal Rest. Celebration. That's what it's all about. Celebration of a life lived to the fullest. We hope. Though there are some—like poor old Gertrude—who never set foot out of Mooreville and never did anything more exciting than pick every one of her prize roses for her sister's wedding.

When Elvis and I arrive, Lovie's in the kitchen stirring the brandied fruit (wearing red), Uncle

Charlie's out front mingling with the guests, and Mama's upstairs practicing her solo. Snatches of "Whispering Hope" waft down the stairs. Every now and then she hits a note that's not in her range.

"Remind me to tell Mama to take that hymn out of her repertoire," I tell Lovie.

"I wouldn't, if I were you. The last time you gave Aunt Ruby Nell advice, she dropped a hundred and fifty dollars at the wheel of fortune."

"Good point. Anything I can do to help in here?"

"No. Go out front and rescue Daddy."

The Latons have arrived, along with a hundred other guests including Mayor Robert Earl Getty and his wife, Junie Mae, wearing a hairdo that looks like it came over on the *Mayflower*. I ease over and put some of my Hair.Net cards on the hall table close to her. Just in case.

Leonard Laton was a prominent citizen, and Uncle Charlie did him proud. A quick glance at the casket shows the chains removed and the late doctor looking almost as good as he did before his cross-country travels in a tarpaulin.

There are other familiar faces in the crowd—the Moffetts, Roy Jessup from Mooreville Feed and Seed, the entire board of Lee County supervisors, Fayrene and Jarvetis, who is making a rare public appearance. He's usually off hunting with his bird dogs. The joke around Mooreville is that Fayrene's husband is as imaginary as her illnesses.

The big surprise among the mourners is not

who's here, but who's not. Jack Jones is nowhere to be seen. Not that I'm looking. Still, I haven't seen him since he backed me up against my beauty parlor sink. It's not like him to miss a chance to mess with me.

I'd be worried if I didn't have bigger things on my mind. Like how to catch a killer. On TV the detectives always skulk around to see who shows up at the funeral and who is acting funny.

Of course, we have the wrong corpse, but still, I believe there's a strong connection between Dr. Laton and Bubbles Malone. I intend to find out what it is, even if it kills me.

Janice is making no pretense of mourning. She's in a wing-back chair as far away from everybody as she can get, filing her nails. If that's not contempt, I don't know what is. In my book that's not far removed from hatred. I'm giving her a large black mark and moving her up two notches on my list of suspects.

Mellie seems to be falling apart. She's standing by the casket bawling, and from her rumpled look I'd say she put something in her tea this morning besides lemon. Poor thing. No wonder. If I had sisters like Janice and Bevvie, I'd take up strong spirits, and maybe even gambling. We won't mention sex.

Kevin and Bevvie are in the doorway greeting guests. He'd look perfectly normal if you didn't notice the twitch in his left eye. Not as damning as

Janice's behavior, but still a tipoff. Something's bothering the usually self-composed Laton son.

There's nothing new to add to Bevvie. She's the same jut-jawed, belligerent woman I saw at the fitness center. Even in a demure navy blue suit she looks every inch capable of killing big game that doesn't feature horns, hooves, and a furry coat. Bevvie tops my suspect list, and I'm not planning to let her out of my sight.

Making sure Elvis is safe (he's over by a floral arrangement of gladiolas charming the mayor's wife), I ease my way toward Bevvie. My progress is slowed by people vying for my attention. Fayrene stops me to ask if Mama's here yet, and Leonora stops me to inquire about Jack. As if his whereabouts are any of her business.

Before I can get within hearing range of murder suspect number one, the front door swings open and in swarm the police. Standing there like somebody has tacked me to the floor, I count five of Tupelo's finest followed by a burly man wearing the logo of the Las Vegas Police Department. He looks like he spits lightning and pees thunderbolts. He looks like he would throw Lovie and me under the jail, then go off and retire to Tahiti while we rot.

I can't get out of there fast enough. Trying to looker shorter so I'll blend with the crowd, I hustle toward the kitchen. Let me tell you, it's hard to run with your knees bent. Furthermore, it's impossible to look short when you're five eight and wearing Jimmy Choos with four-inch heels. I'll be lucky if I don't fall and break every bone in my body.

By the grace of every deity in the universe, I gain the kitchen with everything intact. Except my breath and my sanity.

Lovie drops her stirring spoon. "Good Lord, Callie. What's wrong?"

"It's . . . I'm . . . ohhh."

Mama grabs a cloth, sloshes it in dishwater, and swabs my face. There goes my fifteen-minute personal beauty routine down the drain.

"I'm calling Charlie," she says.

"Wait." I push the wet dishcloth out of my face, blink at the mascara running into my eyes, and try to focus. Grabbing Lovie's fresh broccoli, I dump it from a gallon plastic bag and deep-breathe my way back to partial sanity.

"The police are here. From Las Vegas."

"Oh my Lord," Mama says, while Lovie says a word she didn't learn in Sunday school.

Lovie jerks up the sherry and sloshes it into the fruit, Mama dumps brandy over the cake, and I add vodka to the punch. Then Mama pours us all a cup.

"What are we going to do?"

Lovie's asking me, the way she always does, and I'm fresh out of answers. In fact, I'm fresh out of everything—breath, steam, bravery. Especially bravery.

Right now all I want to do is grab Elvis, run

home, and hide under the bed for the next six years.

Uncle Charlie comes in, takes one look at us, and says, "I see you already know."

Mama hands him some punch.

"We won't let this little incident disturb us, dear hearts. Leonard's services are going to follow in the tradition of fine Valentine funerals since the establishment of Eternal Rest."

Uncle Charlie lifts his punch and we all click cups. *"Laissez le bon temps rouler."*

"What about the cops?" Trust Mama to get to the heart of things.

"The police are very respectful of the dead. They won't do anything until after the services." He puts his arm around Mama. "Ruby Nell, the music will set the tone. Are you ready?"

"I'm always ready, Charlie."

Uncle Charlie and Mama leave to enter the chapel through a side door. Usually I go and sit in the audience out of respect for Uncle Charlie and the dead. Today I decide to sit this one out.

"Listen. Aunt Ruby Nell switched to the organ."

The somber strains of "Whispering Hope" waft toward the kitchen, where Lovie and I are into our second cup of punch.

"That's strange. Mama always plays the baby grand when she's going to sing."

"I guess she's rattled."

Rattled is an understatement. Mama's usually

solid second soprano voice wobbles as she starts the first verse. She thrives on praise and prides herself on a thirty-year record of solid public performance at Eternal Rest.

"Come on, Mama. You can do it."

I know she can't hear me, but I believe heart connections make mind-to-mind communication possible. Her voice grows stronger as she moves into the second verse. *Singing the song of forgiveness* are the words, which I hope everybody who's trying to kill me or put me in jail takes to heart.

Mama's sailing right along, and I breathe a sigh of relief. Then all of a sudden she segues and starts belting out "Blue Christmas."

Holy cow. What's going on?

I race down the hall toward the side door of the chapel to get Mama's attention. And that's when I see him—Rocky Malone, standing at the back of the chapel big as a Whirlpool refrigerator.

Could things get any worse?

I'm waving at Mama from the side door trying not to attract any attention but hers when I spot my dog. Elvis has managed to perch himself near the front with the Laton family, whom he hates. He's probably just waiting for his chance to pee on Janice's Prada purse.

Suddenly he opens his mouth and howls.

I think I will die on the spot.

Elvis' Opinion #10 on
Funerals, Floozies, and Pupperoni

I didn't even get to finish my solo.

There I was, on the front seat minding my own business, when Ruby Nell gave me a musical cue. Now, I've never missed a cue in my life, and I wasn't about to start at this late date. Besides, it was one of my Christmas hits.

If you ask me, everybody would be better off if they'd ditch those funeral dirges and throw in some rockabilly and a bit of Christmas cheer.

I was howling along enjoying the sound of my own voice and the audience reaction, when Callie snatched me up and sailed into the kitchen.

Now here I am with a canceled show.

"Quiet, Elvis!"

She never raises her voice unless she's about to crack under pressure. As much as I hate seeing my human mom upset, I hate missing a performance even more.

What can I say? Artistes have big egos.

I give Callie this hangdog look, which sends her scurrying to the cabinet for a Pupperoni treat. I like Pupperoni as well as the next dog, but a little cake would have been more up my alley.

"I'm sorry, Elvis." She pats my head and I reward her by wagging my tail and licking her hand. "Things are crazy around here right now."

Like I don't know. What does she think I was doing with those hateful Latons? Singing Nat King Cole?

I was keeping my eyes peeled on the suspects, that's what. Planning on soaring to new worldwide iconic status by apprehending the criminal. A first in dog history if you don't count the canine patrol. And I certainly don't. How many of them have ever played to sellout crowds in Las Vegas?

Okay, so maybe I was planning to sneak a piss on Janice's purse, but that doesn't mean I think she's the killer. Kevin and Mellie are the ones to keep an eye on. He's too composed for somebody going through these extraordinary circumstances.

As for Mellie—underneath her ugly clothes beats the heart of a floozie. I know one when I see one. Trust me.

If you ask me—which nobody does—I'd march those two out of the chapel and have Lovie sit on them till they confess.

And speaking of Lovie—here she comes with a hunk of cake, generously laced with spirits. My kind of woman.

"Our little secret," she says. Like I'd tell Callie when she gets back from the bathroom. Like I'd deliberately finish ruining her day.

There are a lot of things I could tell Callie, but I won't. She already has too much on her plate.

For one thing, I'd give her the goods on Rocky Malone. Now, I know he's been chasing around in a Ford F-150 scaring the pants off everybody, but they didn't see what I saw. When Ruby Nell started playing "Whispering Hope," he was standing back there blubbering like a baby. Had this big old white handkerchief he pulled out of his pocket to blow his nose.

A man that tenderhearted didn't knock off Bubbles Malone and toss her in with the frozen fish. I don't know what his role is in all this drama, but as soon as I can make my escape, I'm planning to find out.

And if I don't, my human daddy will.

Don't think I don't know why Jack's not here. Listen, while we were sitting under the stars in Ruby Nell's backyard (unbeknownst to Callie, of course), he told me his plans.

Believe me, he's not missing this chance to watch over Callie so he can whistle Dixie.

Chapter 19

Accusations, Threats, and Honey-Baked Ham

By the time I get back from the bathroom, Dr. Laton's eulogy is almost finished. Over the kitchen's intercom, Lovie and I hear Mama blasting forth on the organ—"Marching to Glory," her hymn of choice to send the deceased rolling down the aisle and through the Pearly Gates.

In this case, I have my serious doubts.

"Quick, Callie." Lovie shoves the sherried fruit at me. "Let's get this food on the table so we can get out of here."

Translated, *before the police and Rocky Malone find us.*

As usual, she's way ahead of me. By the time I get my dish into the reception room (which Uncle Charlie, at Mama's suggestion, decorated to look like the living room in Graceland, minus the shag carpet), Lovie's whizzing back toward the kitchen for the punch. I hope she's adding more vodka. If everybody gets sloshed, maybe they won't notice two desperados sneaking out the back door.

Turning toward the kitchen, I'm getting ready to call after Lovie to doctor up the sweet tea, too, when somebody grabs me from behind and clamps a big hand over my mouth.

251

"Behave and I won't hurt you."

I pop out in goose bumps the size of Arkansas. I know that voice. It's the same one that ordered me to pull over on Cliff Gookin Boulevard. It's Rocky Malone, who wants to kill me.

Not without a fight, you don't. I stomp down with my Jimmy Choos hard enough to ram the spiked heels into his foot. Rocky Malone does not even flinch. I think I'm going to throw up. I'm being dragged off by a mountain, and nobody knows.

Not even Elvis. *Where's my dog?* It's not like him to sit around in the kitchen while I'm being kidnapped.

I bite down on my kidnapper's hand, but I might as well be a fly biting a water buffalo. He just tightens his grip and stalks toward the front door.

As we pass the chapel we hear the drone of conversation, a sign Dr. Laton's been properly eulogized and mourners will soon be spilling out.

Reversing direction, Rocky drags me down the stairs.

Hysteria takes over. I'm fixing to end up on the embalming table. And I can guarantee Rocky Malone does not intend to apply pancake makeup. Most likely, he'll apply the gun I feel sticking in my ribs. I'm going to be Tupelo's latest dearly departed. And I won't even be around to fix my face and hair.

I wish I'd paid more attention when Jack was telling me what to do if somebody ever grabbed me from behind. We were newlyweds, and I thought he was kidding.

"Who would want to grab me from behind? Besides you?" is what I told him, which ordinarily would have led to something fun and maybe even kinky. But he was dead serious.

What did he say? When it comes to beauty, my mind's a steel strap, but when it comes to everything else, it's a garage sale waiting to happen.

Rocky hits the bottom stair, rounds the corner, and heads straight for the embalming table. That's when I remember Jack's advice.

Inching my arms backward, I reach down, grab a handful of Rocky's pride and joy, and twist. He yells loud enough to alert the dead. Unfortunately, Durell Thompson, waiting in the holding room for Uncle Charlie's magic, is not fixing to pop into life and race to my rescue.

And nobody else is, either. This room is soundproof.

It's all up to me. While Rocky's doubled over moaning over his privates, I lunge toward the back door. But just as I get a good grip on the doorknob, he pounces.

"I didn't do anything!"

"Shut up. I'll do the talking." He clamps his hands over my mouth again and pins me against the wall. "I want to know exactly what you and your friend did in Las Vegas."

I'm shaking my head no, but he's not buying it.

Any minute now he's going to lose patience with me and snap my neck like a twig.

"You killed her, didn't you?"

Still shaking my I say, "Ummpft," which is the best I can do with hands the size of Virginia hams clamped over my mouth. I struggle, trying to lift my knee into his crotch, but I'm flattened between him and the wall. Any minute now I expect to hear my ribs crack.

Out of the corner of my eye I see a flash of red. We are not alone.

"Let her go or I'll carve you like a honey-baked ham."

I am shaking with relief. Lovie's standing behind Rocky with the point of a lethal carving knife in his back. And he believes she'll use it. I can tell by the flash of fear in his eyes.

Still, he doesn't turn me loose.

"Hold on, now. I was just asking her a few questions."

"Oh yeah?" Lovie prods and he squeals but keeps me in a viselike grip. "Like you were doing when you ran her off the road."

"I wasn't trying to hurt her."

"Tell that to the devil. That's where you'll be headed after I finish with you."

Holy cow. I've watched Lovie cry over a squashed cricket, and even I believe she's planning to carve him like a roast.

"Turn Callie loose, or I'll cut you. I swear."

"Do what the lady says, Malone, or you'll answer to me."

How Jack entered the room without a single one of us knowing boggles my mind. Or what's left of it. Rocky releases me, and my breath comes back in such a rush I think I'm going to faint. Only curiosity and a determination not to embarrass myself in front of Jack hold me upright.

Elvis skids through the doorway, looking self-satisfied and disgruntled at the same time. If I weren't in my current predicament, I'd laugh. He surveys the situation, then trots over and licks my legs.

Meanwhile Jack is trussing Rocky like one of those yearling calves I've seen at rodeos. Lord only knows where he got the rope. Knowing him, it probably dropped from the sky.

"Are you all right, Callie?" he asks.

"I'd be better if I knew why this man keeps coming after me."

"Rocky is Bubble Malone's son."

Lovie, her carving knife at half-mast, says a word I've never heard. I believe she's taken up cussing in foreign languages.

I'd say a word, too, if I knew any. A big chunk of the puzzle falls into place. I don't know how Lovie and I could have missed it.

We stand back with our arms around each other while Jack straddles a straight-backed chair and points his gun at Rocky. I know a Colt .45 and this is not it. My almost-ex is carrying a weapon big enough to blow the perpetrator clear to California. In the first place, what's he doing with such a gun? And in the second, how could I have been married to a man it turns out I don't even know?

Jack waves his cannon at Rocky. "Start talking."

"When I heard these two women were inquiring about Mother, I followed them to her house. I just wanted to scare them into confessing."

"I can confess to a lot of things," Lovie says, "but murder's not one of them."

"That makes no sense. Why would Lovie and I want to kill Bubbles?"

"I figured one of you had a beef against her since you're in the same profession."

"Pardon?" I ask, and Rocky says, "Show business."

He's quite handsome when he smiles, something you can't tell about a man when he's trying to run you off the road. He's smiling at Lovie now, practically flirting.

"I caught your performance at Hot Tips. Impressive." Good grief, Lovie's preening. "I guess performing's part-time for you, since you live here."

"Au contraire. I perform every chance I get."

Jack prods Rocky with his gun. "Stick to the subject, Malone. The cops are on your mother's case. Why are you in Mississippi terrorizing Lovie and my wife?"

"Estranged wife." If you don't count cohabitation. And I certainly do not.

Jack winks at me. If he hadn't just rescued me, I'd hit him with a can of Freeze and Shine.

"I just wanted to turn them over to the police so they could be extradited and stand trial. I wouldn't hurt anybody. I guess I was unhinged by grief. Poor Mother. When I found her like that . . ."

He chokes up, then pulls out a rumpled handkerchief to wipe his eyes. I don't think hardened criminals do this, but I'm not in a forgiving mood. Thanks to him I have bruises on my arm and two new gray hairs, to say the least.

Plus, I'm indebted to Jack—again—and he's sitting over there acting like my bodyguard from God.

"We didn't kill Bubbles," I tell Rocky. "We just wanted to get Dr. Laton back."

"How'd he get in your mother's freezer in the first place?" Lovie's attitude has softened. She was always a sucker for a sob story.

"I stole the body. It wasn't the doctor who wanted his ashes scattered in the Valley of Fire. It was Mother."

"Why?" I ask. Obviously he didn't kill Bubbles, but maybe he can tell us something that will lead to the one who did.

"It's personal."

"Keep talking." Jack pulls back the safety on his gun.

"What do you want me to say?"

I wait to see if Jack's going to jump in and take over, but apparently he's planning to sit on the sidelines and let somebody else take charge. A refreshing change.

I don't know beans about questioning criminals and perps and suspects—or whatever Rocky is—but I'm planning to give it my best shot. It's either that or end up on the police hot seat with a murder rap.

"Just what was your mother's relationship with Dr. Laton?"

"They had an affair. Even after Mother married, she and the doctor kept in touch."

"The doctor's your father?"

"No. My dad is Flash Malone."

"I'm confused," Lovie finally chimes in. "If you stole Dr. Laton's body, why did you put it back?"

"I didn't put it back. I only carried out Mother's wishes."

Bubbles told us Leonard Laton wanted to be buried in the Valley of Fire. It makes sense she'd ask her son to steal the body instead of doing it herself. He's big enough to steal an elephant and single-handedly tote it across the desert.

"Did you put the pasties in the casket?" I ask.

"Yes. Mother wanted them there."

"You did it again, after Uncle Charlie took the first ones out?"

"Yes, it's not right for a man to go to his final

resting place without a memento of the woman he loved."

"How romantic." Good grief. Lovie's getting moon-eyed, and I'll have to say, I can see why. Now that Rocky's let his guard down, he's nothing but a big teddy bear.

"Was Bubbles dating your father when she had an affair with Dr. Laton?" My question is a shot in the dark. Besides, there's still the riddle of who put Dr. Laton back.

"My father would never have killed my mother. Besides, he's dead."

Well, shoot. There goes that theory. Solving crime is more complicated than making Leonora Moffett look like a natural blonde. How come Lovie's not chiming in?

"Would anybody else you know have reason to kill her?"

"Mother told me that at one time the doctor's wife threatened her."

Great. Another dead suspect.

"Did his children know?"

"I don't know."

If I recall, Dr. Laton had only two at the time. Janice and Mellie. But even if they knew, would one or both of them kill her simply because she was their father's lover?

While I'm trying to figure out what Dr. Laton's affair might have had to do with Bubbles' murder, I glance at Lovie. No wonder she's not trying to solve the crime. She's too busy crossing her legs and hiking her skirt. When I get her alone, I'm going to tell her *come hither* doesn't work when you're holding a six-inch blade.

I poke her with my elbow. Hard. The next thing you know she'll be inviting Rocky Malone to her house for condolence cake and a little undercover work.

Uncle Charlie comes downstairs right in the middle of the fire Lovie's trying to light to report he has explained our mission in Las Vegas to the cops, who have kindly consented to wait until after the interment to question Lovie and me.

"Why do they want to question us?" I ask.

"You were the last to see Bubbles alive. Don't worry, dear heart. I'll be with you."

I'm glad Uncle Charlie's going with us. But the prospect of being questioned by the Las Vegas police in the interrogation room provided by the Tupelo Police Department has me wishing I was born helpless instead of smart. If I weren't the capable kind, Uncle Charlie would never have sent me after the body. I could be home now drinking lemonade.

Satisfied that Rocky Malone is nothing more than a misguided hunk grieving for his mother, Uncle Charlie, Lovie, and Elvis go back upstairs for the funeral reception. Jack unties Rocky, who follows. But not before my almost-ex tells him, "If you touch a hair on Callie's head, you'll answer to me."

I wait till they're gone before I give Jack a piece of my mind.

"If you'd been so concerned about my hair, you'd never have bought that Harley Screamin' Eagle."

That's not all I give him, but I'd as soon forget that part.

I have news for everybody. I don't plan to be interrogated. I'm going to march back upstairs and find the killer.

As soon as I find my underwear.

Chapter 20

True Love, True Confessions, and Dirty Linen

Upstairs I make a beeline for Mama, sitting in the reception room in a corner, of all things. Jack stations himself six feet away looking ready to throttle the next person who looks at me sideways, and thank goodness, Rocky Malone is nowhere to be seen. Come to think of it, neither is Lovie.

When I sit down Mama says, "I've never been so mortified in my life," and I slide my arm around her. "I might as well just give up and become a wallflower."

She's wearing sequins. Neon green and hot pink.

"Trust me, Mama. You'll never be a wallflower.

Besides, nobody noticed. You did such a brilliant segue, everybody probably believes Christmas songs at funerals are now all the rage."

"You think?"

"Oh, I *know*, Mama." She's so relieved I feel better.

"You're right." She stands up and fluffs out her hair. "I might as well perk up and get Fayrene to ride over to Tunica."

Maybe I overdid the pep talk. "Are the Latons back from the interment?"

"You didn't hear Charlie's announcement in the chapel? They didn't have graveside." Mama spies Jack, then gives me the once-over. "Your lipstick's smeared."

"It's not what you're thinking."

"Did I say a word? When have I ever said a thing that's not strictly my business?"

Mama believes her own fiction. Another time I might argue, but right now I have to play hostess . . . and find a killer.

Lovie must have mental telepathy because she pops out of the kitchen and joins us. "Rocky's *definitely* not the culprit, so who put Dr. Laton's body back?"

"If we can find out, we've got our killer. And I think we don't have far to look."

The Laton offspring are hogging the table scarfing down Lovie's liquor-laced delights. All of them, that is, except the youngest.

I don't like this. Bevvie and her arsenal of weapons bear close watching. If she's off somewhere stalking, you can bet your britches it's not white-tailed deer.

"Where's Bevvie?" I ask Lovie.

"She was not here when I came back upstairs."

"I'll work the crowd. See if you can find her."

The mayor and a contingent of hungry Democrats are hogging Lovie's sherried pecan chicken and cheese soufflé, forcing the Republicans to make do with coffee and cake. Fortunately it's laced with enough brandy that they're not complaining.

Kevin, Janice, and her husband, Bradford, have drawn a tight circle at the end of the table away from the mayor's crowd, while Mellie is on the other side, elbow deep in the punch bowl. Judging by her flushed face and disheveled hair, she looks like she's already had three cups too many.

She and Janice act as if they're getting ready to climb across the table and claw each other's eyes out.

I home in on Lovie's brandied cake, making no bones about sidling up close enough to eavesdrop. I don't need excuses. For one thing, I've learned from the expert (Mama at her flamboyant best) to charge forth with boldness no matter what.

For another, Elvis is sitting under the table hoping somebody will drop a crumb. I can always say *I'm here to get my dog.* Not that I'm planning to make him leave.

Listen, this is his funeral home, too. It's partially due to Elvis that we're the *must go to* place when somebody dies. Around here people are fond of saying you can't get to heaven without going through Eternal Rest and consorting with the King.

I lean in to cut a big piece of cake and overhear Kevin saying, "I don't think Daddy looked just right."

I glance around the room hoping Uncle Charlie's not in hearing range. It's not his fault the corpse had freezer burn.

"Who cares what the two-timing old fossil looked like?" Janice says.

Her husband places a hand on her arm. "Now, dear. Don't make a public scene."

"*Me?* I'm not the one getting drunk." Janice twists toward her sister. "And over what, Mellie? An old coot who ruined your life?"

"Leave Mellie alone." Kevin's face is so menacing I take a step backward.

Out of the corner of my eye, I see Jack charging my way. While I'm motioning him to stay on his side of the room, I hear a low rumble coming from under the table. Elvis with his hackles up is a force to reckon with.

"Elvis, quiet."

"Who let that dog in here with the food?" Janice screams.

Elvis makes a beeline for Janice's snakeskin shoes that I wouldn't have. I'm tempted to let him whiz away, but my better side comes to the front and I nab him in the nick of time.

"Did you *see that,* Bradford? I'm fed up." Janice whirls on me. "You Valentines can just go to . . . to *Mooreville.*"

That does it. I've put up with her exploding suitcases and bad attitude, but I will not tolerate any more of her slurs about my hometown. She may consider it the backside of nowhere, but to the Valentines, Mooreville is God's crown jewel.

"You needn't take that pejorative tone."

Lovie bursts out of the kitchen and steamrolls toward Janice, brandishing a barbecue fork.

"Step aside, Callie. I'm fixing to lacerate her liver."

Mama and Uncle Charlie intercept Lovie and escort her to his office before somebody calls Channel 9 and the Valentines end up on the six o'clock news. Meanwhile Bradford leads Janice away. To California, I hope. Permanently.

Then I remember that she's a suspect. I'm tearing after her when Mellie screams, "I might as well die! We might as well all die!"

Everybody in the room freezes.

Is Bevvie lurking around with her lethal weapons? If she is, who will she kill first?

I'm trying to decide whether to look for Bevvie or calm the crowd, particularly the mayor's wife, who looks borderline hysterical, when Mellie falls, face forward, into the punch bowl.

Trying to look in control while Jack pulls her out of the Prohibition punch, I come up with an announcement I hope the crowd believes.

"Everything's all right. She's just overcome with grief. We'll take care of her."

Conversation resumes while Jack and I hustle her into Uncle Charlie's office.

Mama runs into the bathroom for a towel while Jack dumps Mellie into Uncle Charlie's La-Z-Boy recliner. She sits there clutching her purse and shaking.

Lovie's still hanging on to her barbecue fork, just in case, and I'm barely hanging onto my brandied cake.

Grabbing the towel, I try to sponge off the punch, but Mellie's trashing and kicking so hard I'm in danger of being mortally wounded. Just when I'm about to get her under control, Lovie starts jumping up and down, squealing.

"Holy cow, Lovie. What's wrong?"

"Out the window. Quick."

Everybody rushes toward the window—except Mellie, who seems determined to cry the Mississippi River. By the time I elbow my way through, Jack and Uncle Charlie are sprinting out the door.

"She's going to kill us all," Mama says.

She is Bevvie Laton, wearing camouflage. And

she's bending over the open trunk of her car no doubt planning to take out a weapon and blow us all to kingdom come.

While I'm riveted on the parking lot, Mellie clambers out of the La-Z-Boy and heads for the exit.

"Quick, Lovie." She gets there first, and blocks the door while I wrestle Mellie back to the recliner.

From her lookout by the window, Mama yells, "Bevvie's taking something out of the trunk. . . ."

"No, no." Mellie swats at my hands and I motion Lovie to hold her.

If she gets loose in her condition, there's no telling what she'll do. I don't know whether to slap her (I've seen that done on television to cure hysteria) or fix her hair. It's the ugliest mess I've ever seen.

"It's a . . ." Mama says. "Oh my Lord . . ."

Mellie screams and scrambles up again. Grabbing her coattail as she sails toward the door, I feel like I'm in the middle of a three-ring circus. Lovie bars the door again while I drag Mellie back to the chair. She puts her head in her hands and moans.

"What's Bevvie taking out of the trunk, Aunt Ruby Nell?"

"It looks like . . . a camera."

Mellie jerks upright, looking ready to bolt again, and I pat her arm.

"Everything's going to be all right."

"No, it's not," Mellie says. "I should have told Kevin."

"Told him what?"

"Jack's got Bevvie," Mama yells.

"All those years, I should have told Kevin."

"Told him what?" I ask again, but Mellie has stopped talking while Mama won't shut up.

"It's a bomb!"

Mama hits the floor, I dive under Uncle Charlie's desk, and Lovie knocks a wingback chair over trying to find cover. Waiting for an explosion to rock the building, I imagine Jack being blown up. Elvis will be devastated and I'll be a widow. A grieving widow, if you want to know the truth.

And poor Uncle Charlie . . . I don't know if we'll have the heart to carry on at Eternal Rest after he's blown to bits by Bevvie Laton.

Mellie's still sitting in her chair, as calm as you please. Does she know something we don't know?

"Mama, I don't think it was a bomb. There'd have been an explosion by now." I start crawling from under the desk, and she motions me back.

"Stay down, Callie. We're all going to be killed."

"Kevin is Daddy's natural son," Mellie says, and Mama is the first one off the floor.

"Well, I knew it." She looks out the window and resumes her blow-by-blow account.

"Charlie's got the bomb. He and Jack are . . . Wait a minute. Bevvie's loose. She's getting away . . . Oh my God."

Mama sinks into a chair.

"What, Mama? What is it?" I race to the window in time to see Bevvie's car roaring out of the parking lot with Uncle Charlie and Jack in hot pursuit.

I don't know whether to clap or faint. They're chasing a cold-blooded killer who is armed with enough weapons to blow Lee County off the map.

"We need something to settle our nerves." Lovie heads for the coffeepot and pours us all cups that are more Baileys Irish Cream than coffee. Ever the perfect hostess, she passes around linen napkins from the credenza and then we sit there drinking.

In my concern over Uncle Charlie and Jack, I had almost forgotten Mellie. All of a sudden she says, "Mother swore me to secrecy. She told me it would tear up the family if I said anything about Kevin."

"It's okay." I pat her hand, not really caring who fathered Kevin Laton. Still, I feel sorry for Mellie. She's going through a bad time. Plus, it must be awful to be that timid and have a bad haircut, too. "Nobody's here but us girls. You can talk."

"Did they think I wouldn't know? After what they did to me? Did they think I wouldn't find out?"

The Miss Marple in me goes on full alert. I smell motive. And so does Lovie. What if Bevvie's not the killer? What if the killer's sitting right here in our midst?

Lovie and I exchange a look that says *don't scare her off, keep her talking.*

"It must have been awful," I say, not having the faintest idea what *it* is.

"You just don't know."

"Know what?"

Mellie wads her napkin and squashes it into her cup. A large coffee stain blossoms on the linen like cancer. I think Lovie's going to have a stroke.

Then Mellie smiles at us as if we're ladies from Boguefala Baptist enjoying a Sunday social.

"I should have left Daddy wrapped in plastic and dumped him in a ditch."

Elvis' Opinion #11 on
Hot Pursuit, Heroes, and Politics

Well, bless'a my soul. What's that commotion in Charlie's office?

I leave a sizable chunk of brandied cake the mayor's wife dropped on the floor and mosey in that direction. If there's a problem, I need to know about it. As much as I hate to miss what the mayor's saying about garbage pickup and dog pounds, with Charlie gone, I'm in charge.

I always try to be in the know about garbage pickup. They leave a trail of goodies you wouldn't believe. Last month I found a perfectly good ham bone. All it needed was brushing off the coffee grounds.

And listen, I could tell you a few things about the dog pound. That place needs to be torched and something along the lines of a Doggie Hilton erected. Maybe I ought to run for mayor.

Now, there's a thought. But not for today because here comes Mellie Laton running wide open . . . and Lovie chasing her with a barbecue fork. Not far behind is Callie.

"Elvis, stop her."

Here's my chance to be a hero. I put it in high gear and station my fat butt right in front of the double glass doors. I even raise my hackles and show some teeth. Let Mellie Laton get past that if she can.

She tries to make an end run around me, but I streak into her path. Maybe *streak* is stretching it a bit. Let's just say I trot as fast as my stuffed belly will allow.

Mellie comes to a screeching halt, and I'm fixing to grab hold of her knobby ankles when she leaps right over me. Let me tell you, that woman is flying. It would take Superman to hold her.

Back in my heyday when D.J. Fontana was drumming the hell out of that percussion and the Sweet Inspirations were backing me up, I could have caught Mellie Laton in the wink of an eye. But being in this short dog suit hampers me. Not that I'm complaining. I could have come back a cow.

Callie shouts, "She's going for her car."

Lovie races toward the kitchen and comes back with her purse. Then she and Callie whiz past me and fly after Mellie while Ruby Nell puffs down the hall, her hair awry and a smudge on the front of her sequined top.

She never gets mussed. Something serious is up.

Ruby Nell stops in front of the ladies' room and reaches into her purse. It wouldn't surprise me if she pulls out a derringer. That woman is ready for anything.

But no, it's just a cell phone.

"Charlie, come quick. Mellie Laton's fixing to kill us all."

Chapter 21

Showdown, Tell-All, and Fishing

Mellie's already racing from the parking lot in a brown Toyota as plain as her shoes. Lovie and I jump into her van to follow.

"You think she killed Bubbles?" Lovie is sweating profusely as she closes in on the Toyota, and I'm so hot even my hair feels limp.

"Yes. While she was *holed up in her room,* she was in Las Vegas committing murder."

"She doesn't look strong enough to lift the dead bodies."

"Bevvie probably helped her." Then I remember seeing Mellie in the weight room, working out. Is it possible she did it by herself? "Quick, Lovie. She's getting away."

Mellie runs a red light and Lovie barrels after her while irate drivers screech on their brakes and honk their horns. In movies they use stunt drivers for wild chases like this.

Where are the cops when you need them?

"She's going to get us killed," Lovie says.

"Or kill us." I'm not looking forward to confronting a cold-blooded murderer. But it's either that or end up on the police hot seat as the prime suspect.

"Bubbles was Kevin's mother," Lovie says.

"You don't know that."

"It makes sense."

"If that's true, Rocky and Kevin are half brothers."

"No wonder I was so attracted to him."

"We don't have time for your libido. Quick. She's turning into Ballard Park."

Mellie squeals to a halt, lurches out of her sturdy brown car, and takes off toward the lake. We take off after her, armed to the teeth with Lovie's barbecue fork.

Startled ducks squawk and scatter in every direction. A mean old Muscovy takes exception to our invasion and sets out after us, wings flapping and vicious beak snapping.

Is that a gun in Mellie's hand?

"Lovie, duck!" We hit the ground. Any minute shots are going to whiz over our heads.

"Goose shit."

"What?"

"I've landed in it." Lovie looks at me as if I'm personally responsible for the hygiene of ducks.

"Maybe I made a little mistake about the gun."

"A *little mistake.* Help me up from here. I'm going to kill somebody."

I hope she means Mellie, but I'm not so sure. I give Lovie a hand, then outrun her for the first time in my life. Even in my Jimmy Choos. It's amazing how a ripe smell can inspire a person. Not to mention a mad Muscovy. He's bearing down on us, and I don't think he wants to be petted.

"Stop!" I yell at Mellie, and she yells back, "I didn't mean it."

Mean what? To kill Bubbles? To put the linen napkin in the coffee?

She's cutting across the levee where the ground is smoother, and I gain on her.

"Wait, Mellie. I just want to talk."

Without breaking stride she calls over her shoulder, "She stole Flash."

"Who's Flash?" I yell, but she just keeps on running.

I don't think I can do this by myself. I don't know why I didn't call for help earlier. Confusion, I guess. Or maybe pride. Glancing over my shoulder, I yell, "Lovie, call the cops."

But she's too busy fending off the Muscovy with her barbecue fork.

"Shoo! Get back or you'll be pressed duck."

She means it, too. If that duck had any sense, he'd run for his life. Instead, he keeps flogging Lovie.

Meanwhile, Mellie rounds the lake on the east side and stops. With her shoulders sagging and her ugly hair sticking out every which way, she looks like she's lost and can't decide which way to go.

I plow ahead, closing in. Suddenly Mellie turns and plunges into the lake.

"Mellie, wait."

She never looks back, just keeps swimming. Now what? Lovie's on the other side of the lake, but I don't know the situation with the duck and I don't know if she'll notice Mellie in the water. And what if Mellie turns and heads toward the north end? Or the levee?

My purse is at Eternal Rest, my cell phone's in my purse, and I'm in a pickle. There's nothing to do but go after her.

But I'm about not to ruin my Jimmy Choo shoes.

I'm taking them off when Mellie calls out, "I might as well die," then disappears under the water.

I plunge in and start swimming. "It's going to be all right. Come back up . . . Mellie?"

Racing to the spot where I think she is, I dive under and try to find her, but the water is murky and I can't see a thing. I come back up for air, swim a few feet farther, then dive again.

I see an arm, a shoulder, a white face surrounded by tacky hair. Is it too late?

Grabbing her around the middle, I struggle to the surface. Mellie sputters, then starts clawing and kicking, and we both go back under.

If I don't let her go I'm going to drown. But if I do, she'll commit suicide right under my nose. With Herculean effort I drag her to the surface again, then hit her hard enough so she stops fighting.

"Do you need any help?" Lovie's standing on the bank in her blouse and her slip, still holding the barbecue fork. The Muscovy is nowhere in sight.

Either he had the good sense to run or he's on the ground with his neck wrung, waiting for the stewpot.

"I've got her." I struggle to the bank, panting. If Mellie takes off running again, I don't have enough wind to run after her.

Thank goodness, she just sits on the ground with her head in her hands.

"Where's your skirt?"

"In the garbage can. I'll never get the goose shit out." Lovie plops down beside me. "Good job, Sherlock. Did she confess?"

"I didn't mean to kill her," Mellie says.

I give Lovie this look, and she groans upward, then walks off. To call the cops, I hope.

"I just wanted to scare her and make her sorry she's ruined the Laton family."

"Did Bevvie help you?"

"No. I did it." Mellie sits up and squares her shoulders. "Things got out of hand. She started scratching and clawing. I had to defend myself."

"How did you kill her?"

"I grabbed the brass lamp and hit her. When she didn't get up, I tried to hide her body, and that's when I found Daddy in the freezer."

Mellie picks up a big rock and stares at it as if she's seeing a foreign object. "What could I do but bring him home? I wasn't about to let that floozy have him, too."

"Too? Who else did she take?"

"Flash Malone. My fiancé."

No wonder I got goose bumps from the picture of Mellie's escort at her senior prom. It was Flash Malone, Rocky's father.

Mellie gets quiet, and I break out in sweat beads the size of South Carolina. It occurs to me I'm sitting there with a murderer. Any little thing might send Mellie into hysterics or flight or—heaven forbid—another killing rage that features the big rock in her hand.

In the distance I hear sirens. I hope Mellie doesn't notice, and I hope the police are heading this way.

"Daddy got that tart pregnant, and she insisted on having the baby. Mother took Janice and me and left, but he begged her to come back. And she did. The fool."

"Then they adopted Kevin?"

"Bubbles was only eighteen. How was she going to take care of herself and a kid?"

"Exactly. And on a showgirl's salary."

"She never got over losing Daddy and Kevin. In a fit of remorse and revenge, she stole my fiancé."

Back at the funeral home, Mellie was right. Kevin should know he has a half brother. But this family secret is not mine to tell.

"Look at me. Who would have me besides big-hearted Flash Malone? After Bubbles stole him, do you think anybody else was going to have me? When that floozy ending up stealing Daddy's money, too, it was the last straw. I wanted to make her pay, but I never meant to kill her."

After all this is over, I'm going to give her a full makeover. If she doesn't turn on me and kill me first.

"Mellie, do you want to come with me?"

Jack is standing behind us looking like some dark avenger who dropped out of the sky. I'm so relieved I could kneel at his feet and polish his shoes. Among other things.

Tomorrow I'm going to hate that he's the sneaky kind, but today I'm going to go home and light a candle.

Police cars squall to a stop at the top of the hill, and Jack puts his arm around Mellie and leads her off.

The way Mellie smiles at him, you'd think he had proposed. Which is Jack Jones all over. A charming rogue who can lead anybody down the garden path.

Anybody, that is, except me. As far as I'm concerned, Jack Jones' corn has worms, his beans have blight, and his squash has root rot. And I'm not even going to discuss his tomatoes and cucumbers.

Uncle Charlie and Mama arrive on the heels of the cops.

Mama falls on me like she hasn't seen me in thirteen years. "If anything has happened to you, I would die." Apparently she's not all that close to death's door, because when she straightens up, she's full of feist and devilment. "I should have cut Mellie's gizzard out when I had the chance."

"Good grief, Mama. You sound serious."

"How do you know I'm not?"

I don't want to know. I've had enough of murder and mayhem. Instead of encouraging Mama with a reply, I march around the lake to get my Jimmy Choo shoes.

When I get on the other side, I look back and see Mama and Uncle Charlie and Lovie, all lined up in a row watching me, checking to make sure I'm safe.

I grab my shoes, dash a little tear out of my eye, and race back to my family.

Suddenly it hits me. This case may not be over.

"Did Bevvie get away?"

"Jack and I let her go. She had no timing device in her camera and no plans to blow up the funeral home. She was headed to the cemetery to take pictures so she could reassure herself Leonard was six feet under."

"How do we know she wasn't involved? Mellie said she killed Bubbles by herself, but she could have been lying."

"Jack checked Bevvie's alibi. It was airtight."

Jack again. How does he know all that stuff, anyhow? If I were still officially married, I'd try to find out.

"Fayrene said she had some fresh bait." Uncle

Charlie puts his arms around Lovie and me. "After we get you two back home, what do you say we all go fishing?"

It's the most sensible idea I've heard in weeks. I'm so happy to be doing something normal, I'd gladly jump in the lake and spear a fish with the heel of my favorite Jimmy Choo shoes.

Elvis' Opinion #12 on
Diets, Astrology, and Normal

Considering the major role I played in appre-hending the criminal, you'd think folks would show some appreciation. But *oh no.* Now that she has time to notice such things as the portly figure I cut, Callie has put me on a diet. Never mind Ann Margret's opinion that I'm God's gift to poodles.

No Pupperoni. One measley doggie bone a day and no more scraps from the table. If it weren't for Lovie sneaking me a few tasty tidbits, I'd be crying in the chapel.

And speaking of Lovie . . . this Rocky Malone dude has her all shook-up. It turns out he's an archaeologist who's far more interested in old bones than in running women off the road. Heck, he wasn't even carrying a real gun. It was a plastic Roy Roger's six-shooter.

Now that the police have released his mother's body, he has gone back to Las Vegas to make funeral arrangements. But he's been calling Lovie.

It seems he was a tougher nut to crack than Callie thought. He was holding out about what he knew regarding Kevin and his mother. After Mellie knocked Bubbles off, Rocky found a scrapbook in her closet featuring Kevin—school pictures, report cards, hair from his first cut, all the stuff mothers keep, obviously supplied by the doctor. He was quicker than Callie to catch the family resemblance.

Lovie didn't have the same compunction as Callie about telling Laton family secrets. Rocky's coming back after the funeral so he can get to know his half brother.

And not coincidentally to take Lovie out. She told Callie they're having a first date a week from Saturday night.

Lovie doesn't have dates. She has affairs.

You can understand why Callie is confused. When she asked what had happened to Lovie's attraction to Champ, she said, "I've found bigger fish to fry."

As for the Latons, Kevin finally gave up on Lovie, Mellie's facing extradition to Las Vegas, and Janice and her brood are back in California. I'd like to report I have the place all to myself, but it turns out Callie's named that silly cocker spaniel and put another doggie bed in the house.

On the opposite side of the bed, thank you, thank you very much, or I'd have to put out a contract on him.

If she thinks I'm going to take up singing duets simply because she's calling him Hoyt, she's whistling Dixie. Just because I hung a portrait of the Jordanaires in the Trophy Room at Graceland doesn't mean I'm fixing to start sharing the limelight here in Mooreville, Mississippi. I have better things to do than try to teach an untalented stray how to sing.

Now that things are back to normal around here (if you don't count Hoyt, and I most certainly don't), Ruby Nell has motored down to Vicksburg to check out the riverboat casinos. She talked Fayrene into going with her. And guess what else she's taking? The switchblade she keeps in her purse. Nobody knows about it except Charlie and me.

Don't ask how I know. I get around. Anything that's worth knowing, I sniff out.

While Fayrene's gone, Jarvetis is in charge of Gas, Grits, and Guts. Now, there's a man who understands his hounds. I'll be feasting on bologna rinds and pickled pigs' lips if he can get some shipped up from Scooba. And if I can find the back door open.

Callie is back to dispensing beauty and consulting the stars. This morning while we were having breakfast in the gazebo she said, "Listen to this, Elvis." Then she read her horoscope.

Today you're going to meet the man of your dreams.

I don't usually put much stock in such things, but last night while my human mom and I were outside communing with the stars, Venus was lined up with Mars. Let me tell you, when those two powerful planets get together, anything can happen.

For instance, here comes my human daddy on

his Harley. Callie looks out the window, then around at her empty beauty parlor.

"Man of my dreams, my foot. More like my worst nightmare."

Jack strides in and tosses his helmet on the love seat. Well, bless'a my soul. He left the front door open.

I mosey in that direction but my human parents are too busy to notice. She's astraddle him on her own beauty shop chair.

Don't think I'm going to divulge details. I pride myself on being a dog with class.

Nosing the door back, I squeeze my fat butt through and sniff to see which way the wind's blowing. Is that the succulent scent of pigs' lips?

After checking the road for Peterbilt rigs, I trot off to see if Jarvetis is in a sharing mood.

Elvis has left the building.

Center Point Publishing

600 Brooks Road ● PO Box 1
Thorndike ME 04986-0001 USA

(207) 568-3717

US & Canada:
1 800 929-9108
www.centerpointlargeprint.com